Alpha King's Captive

Shifters of Clarion

Lila Bosch and Ariel Renner

Copyright © 2024 by Lila Bosch and Ariel Renner

www.arielrenner.com

All rights reserved.

No part of this publication may be reproduced, distributed, or transmitted in any form or by any means, including photocopying, recording, or other electronic or mechanical methods, without the prior written permission of the publisher, except as permitted by U.S. copyright law.

The story, all names, characters, and incidents portrayed in this production are fictitious. No identification with actual persons (living or deceased), places, buildings, and products is intended or should be inferred.

Contents

Chapter One – Crystal	1
Chapter Two – Leon	13
Chapter Three – Crystal	32
Chapter Four – Leon	47
Chapter Five – Crystal	54
Chapter Six – Crystal	68
Chapter Seven – Leon	82
Chapter Eight – Crystal	90
Chapter Nine – Leon	99
Chapter Ten – Leon	112
Chapter Eleven – Crystal	121

Chapter Twelve – Leon	133
Chapter Thirteen – Crystal	151
Chapter Fourteen – Crystal	166
Chapter Fifteen – Leon	175
Chapter Sixteen – Crystal	182
Chapter Seventeen – Leon	192
Chapter Eighteen – Crystal	201
Chapter Nineteen – Leon	208
Epilogue – Leon	215
Special Preview – Alpha's Arranged Marriage	221
Free book from Ariel Renner	232
About the Author	233

Chapter One — Crystal

"And they lived happily ever after in Wonderland."

A smile tugs at my lips as I finish the story. Alex's cherubic grin fades a little, his eyes heavy, as he loses his fight against sleep. I release a sigh, lean back against the chair, and just watch him as he drifts off. This is the beautiful part about being in the children's ward. The innocence and obliviousness of the harsh realities of the world are disarming. It's such a shame Alex goes through so many pains each day as he battles cancer.

It's funny how bedtime stories are a perfect way to end the day for most children and also the perfect way to bribe a little boy who hates shots. Alex and I have a longstanding deal that if he agrees to his shots, then I'll read him a bedtime story. Works every time.

"Lucky you," I whisper as I adjust the cover over his small body. The silence in the room is only disturbed by the incessant beep of the machine monitoring his vitals.

I can't remember ever having a reason to smile while growing up. My life started in an orphanage. I didn't know who my parents were, but I was told that I was left on the doorstep of the orphanage with a note to take care of "my little bird." The beginnings of my life read like a Dickens novel right from the very beginning. The nuns cared for me there, but there was no love. No hugs for a job well done. No bedtime stories to tuck me in. I was one of many little faces looking to be adopted by any number of kind adults who came into the orphanage from time to time.

I was also one of the few who were never adopted. By the time I was a teenager, I'd given up on that dream and I was just waiting to age out of the system. My life has never been easy. Maybe that's why I went into pediatric nursing. It's the least I can do for children who get a rough break in this life. I guess some might say that a kid like Alex has it worse at eight than I ever did, but I figured out a long time ago that there are no prizes for getting harder breaks in life.

I close the book and silently hope that Alex never stops believing in fairy tales the way I did when I was little. The cold, ugly world can wait for now. Little boys deserve to hold on to their innocence as long as they can.

I quietly leave the room and shut the door behind me. The clean and colorful walls of the ward greet me as I walk down the hallway toward the locker room. It's late in the ward and there's a sort of eerie calm as I make my way. The smell of disinfectant and the faint scent of despair hangs all around me. The hospital administration has done their best to make this place less scary for the little ones. In this part of the ward, there are several murals along the walls with rainbows and frolicking unicorns. As nurses, we even wear scrubs with children's characters on them and doctors never wear their white lab coats here. I've heard that it's because of some Pavlovian response to pain and the sterile clothing that hospital staff usually wear. I don't know if the teddy bear scrubs I have on make any difference, but the way I see it, these scrubs cost the same as the plain, drab ones and kindness is free.

I spot one of my colleagues at the end of the corridor, walking by as she shrugs into her Winnie the Pooh lab coat.

"Alicia?"

She starts and turns to me. Her cat's eye glasses are crooked on her nose. She adjusts them and smiles at me. "Crystal, I thought you left."

"No, I had a last-minute check to do," I reply as I join her at the end of the corridor.

"Good for you. I just started my shift five minutes ago, and now I have to be at the emergency unit," she says with a downcast look. I chuckle at this. Alicia is this thin, frail thing with curly brown hair tied back into a bun. She looks more librarian than nurse and she certainly acts like it. She's got to be the only nurse I know who hates the sight of blood; sometimes I wonder what she is doing in this profession—I guess I'll never find out.

"You have all my best wishes," I say with a pat on her shoulder.

She arches her brows before we both burst into laughter.

"Thanks, I think. I just hope whatever is waiting for me won't have me wishing I was working in pediatrics like you."

"Be careful what you wish for. It's not all roses here, believe me."

She nods and we share a moment of silent reverence for the reality of this job. "Well, I need to rush," she says. "Dr. Manning's a bear when I'm late."

"All right, see you around," I call out before she leaves.

I make my way to the locker room and there's no surprise that it's empty at this time of night. Either everyone has left, or they haven't finished their night rounds. The rows of lockers, the benches, and the showers around the corner are my only company tonight. I'm glad for the privacy because it gives me time to deflate a little from the stresses of the day. Being a nurse always puts me in danger of bringing the drama home with me. At least when I'm here alone, I can get some meditative peace.

I open my locker and take out my street clothes—a plain brown midi-dress with short sleeves and a little sash around the waist. It's nothing to write home about. Simple and comfortable, just like my life. I take off my scrubs and stuff them in the dirty laundry bag I keep in my locker, then change into my simple dress. There's a mirror behind me, so I take a second to look at myself in it just to make sure everything is in place.

It is. There I am in all my glory. Short, or petite as they say, curvy hips and nice respectable breasts that sit perky under my dress. My skin is what one might call "olive," or maybe they might call it tan if I ever decide to go blonde. My light purple hair is up in a ponytail and pulled away from my face—which, by the way, has always been a little too round for my tastes. Looking at my big, gray eyes and full lips, I've always thought that there was model potential there somewhere . . . if only my face was a little thinner. I always wanted those mile-high cheekbones you see in fashion magazines. I guess it's not meant to be.

I turn around and grab my things. This has been the same routine for me every evening since I was hired on at St. Paul's three years ago. Clock in, get dressed, do my job, clock out, get dressed, rinse, repeat.

With my purse in tow, I close the locker room door and leave. As I open the door, I nearly knock Cassandra in the face as she passes by. She steps out of the way just in time and gives me a death glare of disdain.

"Sorry," I mumble as I step out of her way, making my way to the reception area. I can feel her ugly stare on my back. Lily just happens to be sitting there as I walk up. She smiles up at me.

"Going home already?" she asks in her perky, cheerleader voice. Lily is blonde and pretty and deceptively intelligent, which pisses everybody *but* me off most days. I nod in response and I see her slyly look behind me at Cassandra, who's stalking away, her heels echoing off the walls.

"Too bad you missed," she says with a smile. "Somebody needs to clock her one."

"Careful, I hear evil bitches have super-hearing," I say with a chuckle. That catches her off guard, and she laughs and covers her mouth.

"Good one. Be careful on your way home. I hear it's supposed to rain."

"I will. Thanks. Have a good night."

Home, I think as I walk out of the hospital. My tiny, empty apartment is far from the idyllic version of a home . . .but it's mine . . . such as it is. Not that I talk about any of that with my coworkers.

The cold night air hits me as soon as I step outside. Lily was right. The weather is about to turn. I can smell the rain in the air. Good thing I don't live far. I pull my jacket tight around me as I look around the parking lot. A strange, uneasy feeling comes over me. Maybe it's the night air. Maybe it's the fact that two of the three street lights around the parking lot need to be repaired and are now flickering in different spots over the lot . . .

Whatever this feeling is, I'm pushing it aside. My apartment is only two blocks away, and I'd like to get out of this cold and into a warm bath as soon as possible.

As much as I try, I can't shake this gut feeling that something is wrong. It's tightening around my belly like a belt. I quicken my pace as I walk across the lot.

I ignore my dreadful feeling and focus on getting home as fast as possible. The cold is creeping in through my jacket, making me shiver a little as I walk. I get to the street and look down the road at the shadows around the single cones of light shining down on strategic spots on the sidewalk. I fold my arms against my chest, the cold seeming to come from all around me. It's the wrong season for snow, but it's almost cold enough for it.

I pick up my pace as I make my way down the block. A creeping feeling on the back of my neck makes me look around, expecting to see someone on the street with me. I don't see anyone in the light or any figures in the shadows. As far as I can tell, I'm alone . . . yet it doesn't feel like it.

My heart thunders against my chest as I take a sharp turn at the corner. The street is deserted, hastening my steps. The houses lining each side of the road are eerily quiet. Even though it's nighttime. It's not like it's midnight or anything. I can still see some houses with lights on in the living rooms.

I keep my focus on getting home as I count each step. Another block and a half and I'll be in my apartment and in some warmth. That bath is sounding better and better right about now.

"A hot chocolate will be an excellent treat for me," I mumble while trying to shake off my nervousness. The thought of hot chocolate makes me smile. You can sell my soul for a cup. I'm still musing about this when I hear it—a pan clatter behind me. I stop and slowly turn around. If there were any doubts I had that I wasn't being followed, they dissipated at this. I stare down into the street, but there is no sign of life.

I feel it in my guts that I need to get away from here as fast as possible. I breathe in sharply before slowly turning around. I hold my bag tightly and start running to my house. I don't care if I seem crazy, but I'm not about to take any chances. For all I know, whoever it is could be a psychopath or something. My lungs are on fire as I keep running. I don't stop as I reach the second block.

"One. More. Block. To. Go." I take each word one after the other, using them to reassure myself that whatever I am feeling will soon pass, gasping for air as I press on. I stumble to an abrupt halt when a man appears in front of me out of nowhere.

"What the hell?" I gasp in shock. The man is wearing a cloak that covers him from head to toe. I can't see his face because his head is bowed, but everything about him is screaming danger.

I take a deep breath and sidestep him, trying to ignore him completely. As soon as I move, he mimics my movement, blocking me.

"Um . . . can I help you?" I stutter as I come to an abrupt halt. Only a few feet separate us, but his presence sends chills down my spine. He says nothing. He just stands there with the shadows covering his bowed head.

"I need you to stay out of my way," my voice comes out raspy and shaky. Is he deaf? Or just trying to menace me? I take another step sideways, and he does the same, ensuring that he remains on my path.

"This isn't funny anymore. I need you to stay out of my way, or I'll call 9-1-1," I say, trying to sound as firm as possible, but even I can hear the fear in my voice. I swallow hard and wait for him to back away. He still doesn't move.

I reach into my purse for my phone, taking tentative steps backward. The cloaked man keeps advancing toward me, matching me step for step. Sweat drips down my neck even though it's a chilly night. My movement becomes more frantic as I search for my phone.

"Please, stay away from me," I plead, but he doesn't respond. Save for the fact that he's moving toward me, it's almost like he doesn't know I'm here. His head remains rooted to the ground as he keeps advancing. I'm halfway between the hospital and my apartment, but I can't have this psycho knowing where I live. My best bet is to return to the hospital as fast as possible.

I'm about to break into a run when he suddenly raises his head. The moonlight shines across his face, and I stumble in shock. *Holy shit.*

"What in heaven's name are you?" I whisper in shock. My legs have turned to rubber as I try to move away without falling over. There is no way what I'm staring at is human. His face is decorated with scars, and his eyes are as red as fire. His lips are slightly parted, with his canine teeth longer than any I've ever seen. They are sharp and look like they are intent on tearing me apart. This . . . this beast is towering over me, blocking out what little light there is around us.

My pleas stop as the words get lodged in my throat. I mindlessly shake my head, hoping that this nightmare before me will disappear. That isn't going to happen as this beast keeps advancing toward me, and he is closing in on me.

Run. I have to run. I have to—

He stretches his hand toward me. I scream reflexively as my instincts finally kick in and pull me out of my stupor. I'm running mindlessly, my only thought on getting to safety. I hear his heavy footsteps behind me, matching my speed. *Oh, God. Someone help me! Someone please!* I look back, and to my surprise, the beast isn't running at all. He's only walking, but he's about to reach me. I yelp as I try to run faster, but it's too late. I feel the tight grasp of his hand as he grabs me by the scruff of my neck.

"HELP!" I scream hysterically. He turns me around, and now I'm directly looking into the beast's face. My eyes start to burn with tears as he growls like a lion, his mouth turning up in a sneer.

"Please," I focus on begging for my life. My face is wet with my tears as they blur my vision, perhaps trying to save me from the horror I'm face-to-face with. He lifts me up like I weigh nothing.

"Don't kill me. I beg you," I sob, but this beast merely studies me. Maybe . . . maybe he won't hurt me. Maybe my tears, my cries are reaching him.

He opens his mouth wide and pulls me sharply to him, clamping down into my neck. I scream and struggle, the strength of my voice strangled by his grip on me. I feel my body weaken and I try to grab his arms, claw his face . . . something to make him let go . . .

As everything goes black, my last thought is that I'm going to die here in the cold . . .

Chapter Two — Leon

"Alpha King, these attacks on people are getting worrisome for us," Damien, one of the Elders, says. We have been discussing this matter for only twenty minutes and I can see the agitation amongst the elders. The twelve elders sit around the long table and as their leader, I sit at the head with Dylan, my second in command, sitting stoically at my side. We are currently in the royal room, where the discussion of all Clarion's pressing matters is done. Here is where all things in my kingdom are addressed, including issues amongst my subjects. Normally, this is where I see my advisors or perhaps discuss things with the sheriffs of the many counties within Clarion.

Not today, however. The elders in my council have been alerted to a growing problem. Once the twelve pillars of Clarion are brought into a thing, that is all the indication needed to understand its seriousness.

"In no time," says Elder Belfort, his low baritone matching his wide and round physique, "humans will stop thinking about these attacks as mere animal attacks. We all know the inquisitive nature of humans. Raphael and the other outcasts are becoming a problem, my lord."

My skin tingles at the sound of my brother's name. The mere mention of him invokes a certain cold anger in me. It wouldn't take very much for me to shift just by thinking about him. For all the damage he's done to me and mine . . .

It was easier for him to get at me when we were whelps. When we were small, he had a way of pushing just the right buttons to get me to shift and lose my temper. I guess old habits die hard because just this conversation brings back old feelings of rage that I could easily tap into if I should shift to a wolf.

I don't think I'll forgive him for doing this to our people. Raphael and his group of outcasts have caused nothing but chaos in the human world since they got banished from Clarion. Sometimes, I wish we had killed all of them years ago. They have gotten brazen in their attacks on humans, making supernaturals vulnerable to discovery. A low growl escapes my mouth as the image of Raphael resurfaces in my head. There are so many things I wish upon him.

I take a deep breath and focus on the conversation at hand. All that is in the past. Right now, all that matters is dealing with the damage in the now.

"I understand your worries," I say aloud, "and I've been trying to fish out this betrayal of our world. The Mages are working tirelessly on finding my brother, and I assure you that we are going to put an end to all of this." I'm as frustrated about this as they are. The Mages have tried their best to find Raphael. I can't count the number of times I've been to their chambers. The Mages try to trace Raphael using me because of our blood connection, as I am his twin and he is mine. Who would have thought that my greatest enemy would be my own blood?

"Those are fine words," says Belfort, "but where are the actions? Alpha King, surely you must understand our plight on this issue. Raphael and his outcasts must be stopped.

"I know," I say succinctly. "Elder Belfort, I want to catch Raphael more than you can imagine. He has succeeded in hiding his scent, making it almost impossible to find him. We are waiting for that time he brings down his guard."

There are looks all around the table. Silent judgments, perhaps doubt, from the elders.

"We understand, my lord," Belfort says. "You are a great king, just like your father, and we know you want the best for the people of Clarion. We are just hoping that perhaps it is time we attempt other tactics.

Ah. This is what those looks across the table are about. Clearly, there has been some discussion about this before they came to me. My interest is mildly piqued.

"What other means do you suggest?"

Belfort adjusts himself in his chair, the spotlight on him as the other elders look to him to speak their collective thoughts. "I was hoping that we send some of our men out. Perhaps, the wolf pack—"

I scoff. All this drama and that's their idea? As if I hadn't thought of that before. "You want to send soldiers out to find him blindly? Without any real clue as to his whereabouts? What shall we do, then? Knock on every door? Interrogate every subject? Perhaps we should drag people in and torture them for information."

I see Belfort's face blanch. "No, of course not. I was just suggesting—"

"We may be shifters, Elder Belfort," I say over him, "but we are not beasts. I will not terrorize my own people for the sake of finding Raphael. Besides that, spreading our forces out on a wild goose chase leaves us vulnerable. I will not take that risk."

The door opens suddenly and my attention is diverted. Cid of Celene, the oldest family of Mages in Clarion, walks in with a stern look on his face. Tall and intimidating on a good day, Cid is in his leather armor, sword and gun at his side. I glare at him as he bows and takes a knee under my gaze.

The elders rustle with displeasure. It is rude at best to march into a royal meeting you were not invited to. Dylan stands to intercept him, but I gently touch his hand to stop his progress.

"I apologize for this interruption, but there is a matter of importance that needs the attention of the Alpha King," Cid says without looking up. I feel Dylan's tension as he sits next to me, his fist balling up. The elders have gone silent and are now looking to me for my response.

"Go on," I say. "What is so important that you seek my audience without invitation?"

Cid pauses, but he doesn't dare look up at me. "It's about your brother," Cid says, his voice shaky with nerves. My skin tingles with fierce anger.

"Rise," I command. "Speak your mind."

He gets to his feet and addresses me directly. I can see the urgency in his eyes mixed with the relief of being granted an audience with me. "His presence has been discovered, but only for a few moments," he replies. A ripple of gasps and excited whispers rush through the room. I stand slowly, staring him down as if to pounce on him.

"Where?"

"In the human world." He reaches toward his sword and Dylan stands quickly, ready for any attack. Cid pauses at Dylan's quick movement, then says, "I bring aid from my mother." He reaches into a satchel by his belt and pulls out a white stone. I recognize it immediately. It is the map of the human world, and there is a red dot on the side.

I motion to Dylan to retrieve it. Dylan moves swiftly around me and to Cid, taking it from him. As he gives it to me, Cid goes on.

"This is where we discovered the scent. The mark on it will serve as a guide, my King."

I turn the stone in my hand over and over, smelling the familiar scent of my brother all over it. Finally, after all this time...

I remove the long red ceremonial robe I'm wearing and hand it to Dylan. The only instinct I feel is to run and catch up with Raphael. The burning need to end this all overwhelms me.

"It appears the Moon Goddess has answered our prayers. We will reconvene once I have Raphael's head with me," I address the sages.

They have a solemn look but chorus, "As you wish, Alpha King."

They give me one last bow before Dylan and I leave the room. As soon as I step into the hallway, I allow my bear to take control and I race out of my palace. The sound of bones breaking fills the hallway. The tingling sensation in my body overtakes everything else. I feel the change: golden eyes, my fingernails have been replaced with sharp claws, legs have turned into limbs. The rest of my clothes fall off my body as they become shreds. I hold the white ball with my teeth and sprint out of Clarion.

My body is blazing with fury; I only want to find Raphael. I pass through the shield of Clarion and race into the woods. I feel Dylan in his wolf form running after me, but I don't spare him a glance. I won't allow this opportunity to slip from my hands.

"*Alpha,*" I hear Dylan's voice in my head.

"*What?*" I snap back.

"*We have to shift once we get to the edge of the forest,*" Dylan says. This is when I remember that once we leave these forests, we fully get into the human world. We can't risk them seeing us in animal form. I curse as I realize I'll have to run on foot. It isn't a problem for me since we're faster than any human, but I'm not hunting down a human; I'm after my brother's life.

"I know a place near the edge of the woods where I've stashed clothing," Dylan continues as I race through the trees.

This is one of the reasons I hate the human world. If I were back at Clarion, I would have been in my animal form and reached where we are going faster.

It doesn't take us long to reach the edge of the forest after that. As we stop along the treeline, right before the hazy veil between our world and theirs, Dylan and I shift back to our human forms. It is the same process as shifting to my animal form, the tingling sensation and the crackling of bones as my animal side retreats for my human side. I remove the ball from my mouth and wait for Dylan to shift. Once he shifts, he moves over to a small box hidden in a large oak and produces a bundle of clothing for the both of us.

"Thank you," I say as I take the bundle and unwrap it. "You really are prepared for anything."

"It is my job, my lord."

I'm not a fan of being in human form while we search for Raphael. Maybe I'll escape notice since it's dark. However, the risk of exposing my kind is too great. And walking around naked in the human world is a bigger issue than in Clarion. I hear there are even laws against it, if one can believe that.

I glance at the ball and realize we need to head north. Wordlessly, I take off, running through the veil and into the human realm. I'm eager to settle a few things with that bastard.

As we walk into the cool, rainy night, my mind drifts back to when everything was perfect. As children, we had the best opportunities that were afforded to us. Not just as royalty but in the way our parents raised us. My father, the previous Alpha King, was a stern but protective father. My mother gave us all the love we could ever want. As twin sons, Raphael and I were inseparable. We did everything together while growing up. I would have laid down my life a hundred times for him.

Everything changed when it was time for my father to choose his heir. Everyone thought Raphael would be the one, but the Moon Goddess had other plans; she chose me instead. It's never been for me to understand why. If things were different, I would have proudly accepted my duty and worked beside Raphael if he had been chosen as the next Alpha.

I guess Raphael never saw it that way. He changed from being a sweet and loving brother to one filled with anger and hatred toward everyone, including the people of Clarion. He didn't hide the fact that he felt cheated of the power of the Triad.

And here I am now, a lifetime later, tracking him down for his crimes. My rage for his wayward path is palpable despite the memories of a time that has been lost to me now.

Knowing my brother, if I miss him now, there might be a slim chance of catching him again. I mean, this is someone I've searched for over the years, and he has managed to hide. It's interesting that he should suddenly appear this way after so successfully staying hidden. In the back of my mind, I'm questioning it. Why now? Why show up now after everything he's done against our people? Something tells me that there is something amiss. I know the accuracy of the Mages; hence I don't doubt them if they tell me they felt his presence in this part of the town.

Ironically, it's a town close to Clarion. It makes me wonder if my brother plans to attack Clarion again with his outcasts. The thought of it has me on edge. I can't help but remember the last time this happened. It was what

I've heard referred to as a "Pyrrhic Victory" in human lore. We beat his forces back but lost so many that, at one point, I believed that we would not recover should he try another attack. That was one of the biggest mourning periods Clarion had witnessed. A time of irreplaceable loss amongst my people. I swore I would protect my people's lives after the incident, even if it meant destroying my brother.

I pause when we enter the human streets. As we walk, we soon pass a well-lit healing facility. The heavy scent of chemicals and human blood and waste is thick here. I've only walked past a place like this once or twice in my life and I've never liked it. Humans have strange ways of healing. I ignore it for now and keep my attention on the excitement filling me as I realize we are only a few steps away. We're closing in on him.

I slow my steps when I see the ball's direction lead to a street. The street is reasonably lit by large street lamps and while there are shadows all around this place, there are plenty of houses along the sidewalk. I look back down at the ball questioningly. He's definitely this way. I don't know why Raphael would be out in the open like this . . .

Perhaps he is hiding in the shadows . . . The scent of humans is strong here, though. For all his attacks on them, he's still managed to remain hidden from humans as is our way. Has that changed? Something isn't right. I come to an abrupt halt, scanning the street ahead of me.

"What is it?" Dylan asks. "Do you sense him?"

I don't answer. I'm trying to analyze what my senses are telling me. Before me, just beyond one of the street lamps, is a heap of clothing. I smell human blood. Strong and fresh . . . and I think it's coming from the clothes.

I take a few steps towards it and slowly, it occurs to me what I'm seeing. It's a body. Some human lying in a pool of blood on the concrete. It may be alive or not. I can't tell from here. I stop, frowning in indecision.

"Alpha?" Dylan gives me a questioning look, waiting for my next command as he stops beside me. Normally, we leave humans to deal with human situations like this. But as I stand there staring at it, I feel a pull drawing me closer. I have this uncontrollable urge to approach the dying or dead human.

More importantly the body is where the ball is leading us.

This could be a trap. Coward that he is, I wouldn't put it past him to use a human as bait.

"Is . . . that a human?" Dylan asks me. I nod and put my finger to my lips. There's no telling who is watching us.

I lead the way, moving towards the body on the sidewalk while taking in my surroundings. The air is filled with his scent. Deceit, the evil and vile creature that he is.

Dylan smells it as well. He whirls around, looking through the dark shadows with his preternatural eyes.

We reach the body . . . a woman. I can feel her heat reaching out to me as I stand over her. She is . . . alive.

"He is no longer here," Dylan says with a worried look down at the woman. The news doesn't come as a surprise to me. Obviously, Raphael mistakenly left his scent here when he attacked this woman. My best bet had been to catch him here, but now he is gone.

I focus on the woman as I kneel down to her, my ears picking up, the faint beating of her heart. This is Raphael's work, most certainly.

The woman is lying on her side with her hair covering her face. I don't know if the anger I feel for my brother is causing the tingling sensation I'm starting to feel. This woman's sweet, tantalizing scent almost makes me lose my mind. I reach out and brush the hair from her face. Time freezes as I stare at the most beautiful woman I've ever seen. Her lightly tanned face, her small lips pale pink, full, and plump.

"Bastard," I curse when I notice the deep bite marks on the side of her neck. If I had any doubts about who did this, this mark's all the proof I need—it belongs to my brother. My brother's fangs are only second in size to my fangs. No one else has fangs as big and long as this but him. I can't explain it, but I see red as I watch this woman fight for her life. The overwhelming need to hunt down that bastard and tear him limb for limb almost makes me lose it.

What puzzles me is why Raphael had fished this woman out. I can swear that this meeting isn't coincidental. I know my brother would have killed her if he wanted to, and it's not a coincidence that she was left half-alive.

Raphael has brutally killed a lot of humans for years, but never has he just left them alive with only a bite. There must be something about her. Bite marks are sacred in Clarion. It might be one of the few things Raphael respects about our laws.

"Alpha King, what do we do?" Dylan asks. I'm unable to tear my eyes off this fascinating woman. For some unknown reason, fear trickles down my spine at the thought of her losing her fight to live.

I hear Dylan gasp in shock as I shift my hands beneath her body and lift her up. She is so tiny and fragile. Only a beast like my brother would harm this kind of person.

I feel my bear, lion, and wolf forms stir as I cradle this beauty. Each of them wants to be let out. They long to reach out to this woman in my arms.

"Let me carry her," Dylan says as he moves to take her from my arms. I see red and growl angrily at him. The protective instinct in me is at its full peak.

Dylan's eyes widen as he stares between me and the beauty in my arms, clearly in wonder as to my actions. Even if we had the time, I don't think I would have the words either. All I know is that we need to get her to safety.

"We need to get to Clarion immediately," I tell him.

"Clarion?" Dylan exclaims. "But, my lord, she is a human."

"She also needs help, something her people won't be able to provide given how lethal my brother's bite is," I reply. I nod towards the discarded bag along the curb. Her things are all spread out. "Grab her things," I command.

Despite Dylan's displeasure, he does as I instruct. Gathering everything up and putting them back in the bag. He stands, holding it in his hands.

"My lord, I do not mean to question your authority, Alpha King, but the risk of bringing this human back with us—"

"What do you think will happen when some human comes along and finds her like this? What do you think they will do with her when they take her back to their healing facilities? We risk revealing our kind if her people see her with these bite marks. There will be questions we don't want them asking," I counter irritatedly.

"But, my King—" Dylan starts to say.

"Are you challenging me?" I growl instantly. Dylan bows his head.

"I would never think of such a thing," he says, but it does nothing to appease my anger. First, my brother managed to slip from our fingers—again leaving a half-dead woman in his wake. It's even more puzzling that she is the only one he attacked.

Without saying another word, I adjust this fascinating woman in my arms and take off. Dylan joins me and runs after me. Carrying her makes me a hair slower than normal, but that's just as well. I don't want to add to her injuries. Frankly, it's amazing that someone as tiny as she is survived my brother's bite.

A growl escapes my lips when she whimpers in pain. I stop and hold her with one hand. I can see her clearly even though we are in the dark part of the town. I can't help it as I caress her face to soothe her. Her eyes are still shut, but her face is contorted in pain. I grab her tiny hand and find myself caressing it. I think I've lost my mind—why else am I reacting this way to this female?

My animals stir, wanting to break loose. My tongue aches to clean up her wound. I can feel the swollen tissues in my tongue throb. Another groan escapes her lips, sending a sharp signal to my heart.

I growl, feeling more helpless than I have felt in years. The last time I felt this way was watching my parents breathe their last. A tortured growl tears from my mouth before I can help myself. I watch Dylan's eyes briefly widen as he glances at me.

"My King?" Dylan asks, worry in his voice. I glance at her again; I want to reassure her. However, I don't know how to. The best thing is to get to Clarion fast.

"I'll shift to my lion form; I want you to gently place her on my back," I order.

He looks around tentatively, clearly worried about us being revealed should some human see us. I don't care. I expect him to obey my orders.

"Make sure you don't rest her weight on the side that hurts her badly," I tell him.

She must not die, this woman. I have to do what I can to preserve her life. Shifting to my lion form is the most painful, perhaps because it is my largest form. My bear and wolf forms are bigger than anyone else in Clarion, but my lion form is gigantic. But the choice is intentional. I can carry her easily for the rest of my journey this way.

I grimace in pain as the crackling of bones begins. I shut my eyes as I allow everything to fall into place. In minutes, I'm covered in fur. I glance at Dylan, who is watching me with wide eyes. He steps forward to do as I instruct, and a flash of jealousy rushes through me as he touches her. I hold back, however. *What's wrong with me?*

Dylan lifts her up and carefully places her on my back as I've asked.

As soon as I feel her on my back, peace fills me, and I chuff softly. She feels perfect against me. Without another word, I start running. I try my best to be careful with the beauty on my back. I don't know how long we run before we reach the edge of Clarion.

"Alpha," Dylan mind-links with me.

"What about your brother?" he asks. That's interesting. I haven't thought about going after Raphael in these minutes since deciding to bring her back. *Who is this woman who makes me forget my purpose?* I wonder as I keep running. I can feel that there is something more to this in my soul. If there is one thing I know about my brother, it's that he always has a motive for something.

"I'll deal with him later," I mind-link back at him.

I contemplate shifting to my bear form to make my journey faster, but this tiny lady is delicate; I don't think she needs a rough ride. One good thing is that we are closer to Clarion. The bad news is that her heartbeat is becoming fainter.

It pushes me harder to reach Clarion on time. Somehow, I feel that if this woman dies, then there will be hell to pay. I'm relieved when the hazy Mages' shield over Clarion comes into view. To humans, it will only look like the cliff's edge, but behind it is my kingdom.

"Secure the parameters," I mind-link with Dylan as I carry the woman to my home. A human in Clarion—something that has never happened before.

Chapter Three — Crystal

He's coming. My heart beats rapidly as I try to get away from the demon. Perspiration covers my face. I'm losing air, but I keep pushing. I can't let him have me.

"No," I gasp as I keep running down the lonely street, hoping that someone will come to rescue me—but I have no one.

A scream tears out of my throat when the demon grabs me from behind, and his mouth opens wide.

"No!" My eyes spring open and I sit up, covered in ice-cold sweat. I look around frantically, the nightmare slowly disappearing as the waking world comes into focus.

The first thing I notice is the unfamiliar room. Fear grips me as my mind races to the last thing I remember . . . the beast tearing me apart with his teeth. Did any of that even happen?

I glance to my side and wince as pain shoots through my body. Instantly, I raise my hand to my neck and find a bandage neatly wrapped around it. I freeze when I recall how the beast had bitten me at the same spot. Did someone rescue me? If they did, why am I not in the hospital? I take another look at my surroundings and take everything in. It looks like a well-lit cave.

A light hangs in the air near me, glowing, warm and preternatural over my head. It shines brighter than any lamp I've ever seen.

I realize I'm on a massive bed; I don't know how I got here. My clothes have been replaced with a thin night dress. Somehow, I don't think that beast would do something as considerate as this. There are tiny windows lining the walls. I swerve my leg to the side of the bed to get off. I gasp as I step down, the floor giving to my weight like a soft cloud.

What the hell? I wonder if I'm dead and this is heaven.

"Come on, don't be absurd," I say out loud, trying to reassure myself. A dizzy spell hits me when I stand. It causes me to fall back on the bed.

"Damn it," I curse as pain shoots to my neck. I feel a tingling sensation on the wound and instinctively reach to touch it.

I lay sideways on the bed for a moment with my legs dangling over the side. Lying there, my mind tries to rationalize how I got here and where "here" is. After a few minutes, I summon the courage and sit up. I shut my eyes, and this time, I stand up slowly.

I get to my feet without falling and I'm relieved. The night dress I'm wearing falls mid-thigh. I feel lightheaded, but I manage to hold on to the side of the bed for support. I take slow steps to the windows and breathe a sigh of relief when I successfully reach one.

I look through the window and what I see surprises me. I gape as I stare at a large, beautiful garden. There are so many flowers and springs clustered around in almost patterned patches. I count about four springs, wondering how everything is in the same place. It makes more sense that I'm in a cave.

I'm still trying to take everything in when someone says, "You shouldn't be up."

I spin around so fast that it makes me dizzy. I have to lean against the wall for support as a woman stands a few feet away from me by the doorway. I never even heard her come in. Maybe I was distracted by the beautiful sight outside. I take a proper look at the woman. She has long, silver hair and it's the most beautiful color I've ever seen. It seems to shine with its own light and it's so long that it sweeps the floor. Her skin is flawless. Devoid of wrinkles or sags, yet her eyes seem ancient somehow—heavy lidded and wizened. I don't think she's very old . . . but I can't be sure. Maybe she is young and the silver hair is just genetics . . . or else it's a fabulous dye job. I should get her hairdresser's number when all this is over.

"Are you going to keep staring all day, or will you let me apply these herbs to your wound?" she asks as she walks to the bed.

I look down at the bowl she's carrying, and I can't take my eyes off it. It's the most beautiful gold bowl I've ever seen. It's metal or maybe it just seems metal because of the color because there are these intricate flowery designs around the rim. It's stunning . . .

She's just staring at me in silence like I've lost my mind. Maybe I have. Maybe all I think happened was a dream. *What about my neck wound?*

I step away from the wall and walk back to the bed as she comes all the way into the room. I'm still looking around at the strange cave room with the soft, cloudlike floor. It's such an odd place.

I sit on the side of the bed. The way it dips is heavenly; it won't be difficult to lull me back to sleep.

The rational part of me snaps out of my daydream as I focus on the fact that I'm in the same room with a stranger in the middle of nowhere.

"Who are you?" I blurt suspiciously. I don't know who she is or what her game is . . . but I imagine she's not the one who trapped me here. Surely, if she meant to harm me, there was ample time to do that before now.

"I should be the one asking the questions," she says. "Like why did he bring you here for instance? What's so special about you?" A little bit of fear fills me from her tone. It's not harsh or even angry . . . perhaps just a little irritated. Like she was dragged out of her warm bed to deal with me.

But let's not gloss over this implication she's just uttered. "He," I whisper. My breaths become sharp and fast as my mind drifts to the beast.

"Yes." She looks me over, her eyes trying to read me as she peels off the bandage. "You should be grateful that he brought you here in time, else you would have been dead." That's rich. She sounds like that beast did me a favor or something.

"I wouldn't be here if it wasn't for him! I was on my own when he attacked me," I snap in anger.

"Stop talking nonsense. The Alpha King would never attack you," she says. *Alpha King? What kind of name is that?*

"Well, he did," I say defiantly. She raises an eyebrow, pausing as she gathers the herbs from the bowl. "As a matter of fact, he wanted to kill me. Should I be grateful he didn't?" I scoff in annoyance.

"I'd watch my tone if I were you." She puts the herbs on my neck. It stings, so I flinch. "Hold still," she warns. I sit there, letting her press the mixture into my wounds. With a gentler tone, she says, "I can't question the Alpha King's decision, but it would have been better if he left you with your people. Your being here has been quite taxing."

"Well, don't let me keep you," I say bitterly. I let her finish putting the herbs on me. As she replaces the bandage, I ask, "Where are we, anyway? I need to get back—"

She snickers. "You're not going anywhere until you're healed," she says.

I huff bitterly. "What time is it?"

"The sun is at its peak," she replies. She's done bandaging me and she steps back and stares at me as I stare back at her incredulously, waiting for her to tell me the actual time.

"I'm asking about the real time? Is it eight o'clock? Nine?"

Her face splits into a slow smile. "I believe I've answered you," she says. *Smartass.*

"I don't know what the hell is going on, but I need to leave," I say with a raised voice. Her smile doesn't change. In fact, it seems a little cold and completely unfazed.

"I would listen to her if I were you," I hear from somewhere behind her. I look up to see a huge man standing in the doorway. He's so tall he might as well be a wall of a man. As he steps into the light, I can see that he's as muscular as he is tall. He's wearing what looks like a sleeveless leather vest, his massive arms at his side.

He looks like a giant . . . yet there's nothing lumbering in his stance. He moves with an aura of grace.

So. This is the beast that attacked me. I . . . think. I didn't expect him to be so . . . handsome. With his angular-shaped face, finely shaped Roman nose, and high cheekbones, he looks like he could be on the cover of a romance novel holding a half-naked woman in his arms. He sets his amber eyes on me and I feel a warm sensation run through me.

Goose bumps run over my skin as I inhale his woody scent. His hair, black and shiny, is pulled back into a neat ponytail and all I can think about is ripping away the band holding it together and running my fingers through his long, wavy tresses.

As he walks into the room, the light catches his eyes and they seem to change to a golden color, then back to amber. They drift from my face down to the sheer nightgown I have on.

"Pervert," I mutter, more to myself than him. The trance I was under has been broken and now I want to grab the blanket and cover myself to deny him the pleasure of seeing my body.

"My face is up here," I tell him, ensuring that he can detect the irritation in my voice. The silver-haired woman gasps, but I ignore her. My sole attention is on this man who refuses to take his eyes off my body.

His brow furrows and his gold/amber eyes harden. A sharp and primal fear races through me as he stares me down. I don't back down, but my fists are balling up in the sheets under me.

The old woman bows her head deeply.

"My lord," she says. "I was not expecting you this early."

What is this? Is this some weird Middle-Ages kink or something? *How absurd*. I roll my eyes and ignore the fact that my nipples are hardening and my clit is pulsing as though it needs attention under his angry gaze.

"Hannah," he says with a deep voice. It sounds like a purr and my body hums with a sudden need. I don't even want to dwell on the direction of my thoughts.

He says nothing more. She looks up at him for a moment, then nods as if a silent message has passed between them. Without another word, she leaves, taking the golden bowl with her. I want to call out for her to stay. She is the less scary person in the room.

"She won't come back here until I'm done with you," he says as he marches towards me. I scramble backward, trying to put as much distance between us as possible. I'm all the way on the bed as he stops his pursuit at its edge.

"What do you want for me?" I stammer. The anger and lust in his eyes are looking me over, analyzing me. "Are you holding me as a hostage?"

He continues to stare for a moment; the urge to melt under his gaze is almost overwhelming me. I force myself not to look down at his massive chest . . . the aura of power around him is doing its best to draw me in.

He sits down on the bed next to me and he says, "You're not a hostage, but you're not well enough to leave, so you might as well stay and answer a few questions for me."

"I'll do no such thing," I say as I scooch up to the headboard, pulling my legs up to my chest. "Let me go or . . . or I'll call the police."

His face is like stone. I can't tell if I'm intimidating him or not. "You will tell me what I want to know. I won't be denied."

He almost sounds like he's growling at me. It reminds me of the beast in my nightmares and I start to quake inside with fear.

"Where am I?" I ask him, if for no other reason than to stave off the burning in my eyes. "Why did you attack me?"

He tilts his head, his frown deepening. "You think I am your attacker?"

"You . . . you're not?"

He shakes his head. "I need you to tell me what happened to you last night. Exactly what happened."

"Hold on a second," I say, pulling my knees closer to my chest. "How do I know you aren't the one who did this to me in the first place? I don't know what games you're playing with me, but it needs to stop. I need to get out of here."

He sighs and it sounds like I'm pushing whatever patience he has. "I will tell you everything you want to know *after* you have answered my questions."

I shake my head. "This is kidnapping."

"Not here, it isn't."

"Here? Where is *here*?"

He slams his hand on the bed. The mattress rocks violently. I yelp out of fear as he leans into me and, in a low voice, growls, "What happened last night?" I can't speak for a moment, fears seizing me. I don't know what he'll do to me and my feelings are all mixed up inside me. I almost *want* him to show me what will happen if I don't obey him.

I swallow hard and answer him.

"Some weird, scary guy attacked me on my way back from work." I shudder as I think of it. My hand instinctively goes to my neck.

"That's all?"

"Does there need to be more?" He raises his eyebrows at me. I go on. "I was walking home from work and some crazed nut jumped out of the shadows and . . . and bit me on the neck. Hard. And I guess . . . I guess I passed out."

He doesn't say anything. He seems like he's thinking over what I've said. I guess it's my turn for some answers. "How did I get here?" I ask him.

"I found you half-dead on the sidewalk and decided to save you," he explains. That's a little surprising. He doesn't seem like the "saving" type.

Still, I guess I owe him my life.

"Thank you for saving me." A moment passes between us and I start to relax a little. Whatever he wanted to know, I've told him, so . . .

"So, all this is your property," I say. He doesn't respond, so I assume I'm right. "It's beautiful," I add and watch his eyes widen with surprise.

"You haven't seen the half of it," he says, the semblance of a smile tickling the corners of his mouth. I think I detect excitement in his voice.

"There's more?"

"Yes, Clarion is a beautiful place. Large, expansive hillsides with lush, green mountains. Progressive and advanced building structures around the city's center. Anyone would want to live here," he says with pride. *Clarion . . . I think I've heard the name before.*

"I'm sure it's very beautiful," I say as kindly as I can muster. "The little I've seen is . . . well, it's beyond anything I've ever laid my eyes on."

He nods shortly. I've pleased him with my compliment. I'm going to press my luck with him.

"That being said . . . I need to leave. I don't know what time it is, but I'm expected at my job," I tell him.

The kind semblance is gone, replaced with something else. Something darker. "You're not well enough to leave."

"I feel fine," I say and I can hear my voice start to shake a little. He can't keep me here. He just can't. "Listen, I'm a nurse. I can take care of my own wounds just fine. You don't have to keep me here."

"I'm aware of your job, Crystal, but for your own safety, you need to stay here," he says.

"For my own safety," I scoff as he gets up and starts for the door.

"What is this? And just who do you think you are?" I get up from the bed and stand up, ignoring my spinning head. "You're not the hero you think you are if you won't let me leave, you know. Regardless if you saved me or not. I have a life, and I won't allow you to make me a prisoner here."

"Sit down." His command sends shivers down my spine. I gulp as I obey his order, sitting back on the bed.

"You don't know what I've risked to bring you back here," he growls. "I risked everything to keep you safe. I will *not* be berated for that. Now you are in danger from a very terrible, very dangerous creature. Should he come back for you, you might not be so lucky next time."

I'm struck silent, staring up at him fearfully. "He?" I dare to ask. "It's a man after me?"

"Not a man. Raphael is as far from that as any creature in this place." He raises his voice, and it vibrates through me like a roar. "You would not have survived without my help and the help of the Mages here. I will not just send you back out to be ripped to pieces."

Raphael... Is that who attacked me? "Who... or what is Raphael?" I cautiously ask. His face hardens before he says,

"That's not your business. What's important is that I have to protect my people, and if it means having you here for as long as possible, so be it."

My eyes start to burn with tears and my bottom lip quivers. I stiffen it. I'm not going to let him see me weaken. "I won't stay here. You can't make me—"

"You. Will. *Stay.*" He advances on me, towering over me. My heart leaps in my chest as equal parts fear and arousal come over me. "My word is binding. Until I figure out why Raphael has singled you out, you will remain here," he says.

"Fuck you!" spills from my mouth before I can help it.

A low animal growl escapes his lips as he leans into me. "Try to defy me," he says. "Then you'll truly understand why my word is bond in this place."

We stare at each other and I feel more challenged than afraid. I'm so hot I can barely think straight. I want to dare him to grab me with those thick arms of his—*What am I thinking? Snap out of it!* I lower my eyes, pulling away from him. He stands up straight and says, "Here I am king. You'd do well not to forget it."

With that, he turns and leaves the room, leaving me sitting there, my skin on fire and my panties wet. What the hell have I gotten myself into?

# Chapter Four — Leon

I march out of the Mage's cave, furious. My fists balled up to keep my claws from coming out. Fury fills me as I think of how she had challenged me back there. Anyone who has ever dared to challenge me has paid dearly with their lives. I have never walked away from a fight before now.

I stop in the hallway, my heart racing and trickles of sweat rolling down my back. I've noticed I'm as hard as I've ever been, my cock pressing against the buttons of my pants. *What hold does this woman have on me?*

I take a breath to calm myself. It will take time, but she will recognize me as her Alpha. I will bend that will of hers to me before this is over.

Dylan is waiting for me outside. As I walk out, I see him standing on the path, his eyes scanning the area around us. I make my way to him. To think, I was filled with happiness when the Mages sent a message that the strange woman had woken up. I wasn't expecting her to be awake so soon due to the extent of her injuries. I don't think anyone was. Humans don't fare well with animal bites that severe. I'd been told when I brought her here that it would take her at least to the next full moon before she woke, that is, if she survived at all. Who knew that she would prove the Mages wrong?

I need to know what's different about her.

As I walk up to Dylan, I don't bother with any pleasantries. I tell him directly, "I need you to find out as much as you can about Crystal."

"Yes, my King," he says. "My lord, the sages are asking for the outcome of your trip," he adds. I pause, thinking of the futile attempt to catch up with Raphael.

"Alpha King?" I turn to see Hannah coming up to greet us from the cave entrance. "Thank you for coming so quickly," she says with a bow.

"Thank you for doing such a good job with her. I must confess I assumed it would take days before she woke."

"I'm as surprised as you are, Alpha King. Your brother's bite is lethal for a human, but she managed to survive," Hannah says with a pensive look. There's more going on, clearly.

"Speak your mind," I tell her.

She pauses, biting her lip and looking from Dylan to me and back again. "Your Majesty . . . I do not believe the woman is human," she says, and I give her an incredulous look.

"What do you mean?" I ask her.

"The only way a human would have survived a bite as critical as that is if he or she were one of us. I was told she was brought here from the human world?"

I can't make sense of her words. Surely, she can't mean what I think she is saying.

"Of course. I was the one who found her," I tell her. "You know that all of our kind is here. The only people out there are outcasts."

She nods and says nothing to that. Afraid to speak. "Hannah, tell me what you are thinking," I press.

She takes a breath, then says, "I've heard that there are supernaturals like us in other worlds who have homes like ours. What if she is one of them?"

I have never known Hannah to make baseless claims or accusations. She is among the wisest of the Mages that I have ever come to know. I remember her telling me that Raphael had crossed to the dark side, and I needed to be careful. Several moons after, Raphael showed his true colors, and it had been too late for me to save the most important people in my life. Had I listened to her sooner . . .

"What I'm saying," she says, "is that I feel that there is more to this woman. The speed of her healing can only be attributed to a supernatural. Most importantly, a powerful one."

"Powerful," I say, doubts creeping into my spine. She can't possibly mean that Crystal, the tiny girl inside, is *powerful*.

"Did you notice anything else about her?" I ask. "Any . . . abilities or maybe markings that might tell us what she truly is?" I watch her eyes flicker for a moment.

"No, I noticed nothing, my King," she says.

I trust Hannah's word, so I nod and say, "All right, take care of her. I will return to check in soon. Do not allow her to leave."

"As you wish," she says before I leave with Dylan. We're only a few steps down the path before he says, "You should know that the sages have requested an audience."

"I'll deal with it tomorrow. There are matters of the court I need to attend to."

"I can do that, Alpha King," he says. His tone makes me think there is more. I pause, stopping him with my hand.

"Is there something you want to tell me?"

He glances in my direction before diverting his eyes.

"I'm worried, my lord. What if your brother planted this human to infiltrate our fortress?" I think about this for a moment and realize his suggestion is possible.

"More than that, however, her presence has given me reason to worry for you," he says, effectively drawing me out of my thoughts.

"Me? What are you worried about?"

"Your reaction towards her when we were bringing her here . . . or even the fact that you insisted that she be brought here at all. She is a human and humans do not belong in Clarion."

"Hannah just said she may not be a human at all."

"Yes . . . but how could you know that, Sire?"

I frown at him. He's speaking in circles. "What are you saying?"

"What I mean is that . . ." He stops, clearly too afraid to speak it. He sighs resolutely and says, "Sire, what if she is the chosen—" he starts to say, but I raise my hand to stop him.

"No," I cut in. I don't have time for this discussion of mates and fated companions. I have no room for a mate, not after what happened the last time. The Moon Goddess would never be merciful enough to grant me a second chance and I will not hear any hopeful ramblings about such a thing.

"But—" Dylan starts to say and I glare at him to silence him.

"Enough. My mate is dead. I don't know what you think you see in this human or whatever she is, but she is not fated to be mine," I explain to him. "This discussion is moot. Am I clear?"

"Yes, Alpha King."

We make our way to the main road and in the silence, my mind starts to entertain the daft notion that Dylan has just presented. Crystal is not my mate . . . though it would explain my deep connection with her or how my heart races every time I speak her name. And her scent . . . sweet and alluring, pulling me close to her without a word. That argument we had a little while ago made me want her in every possible defined sense. I can see myself marking her as mine.

We walk through the gardens of the Mages, making our way back to the fortress and all I want to do is erase Dylan's suggestion from my mind, but it keeps coming back. My other sides aren't making things easier; they restlessly want me to go back to Crystal.

Her scent is still with me and I can feel the urge to appease my animal sides, letting them take over and bound back to her. I am in control, however, and I have more important things to attend to. I march with fast strides toward the Royal House. Perhaps, if I deal with the problems of my people, I'll be able to take Crystal off my mind.

We pass by Clarion's central homes. I'm glad to see my people enjoying the peace they deserve. I still don't understand why Raphael would throw this life away for his selfish desires.

They bow as I pass, and I acknowledge them with a nod. All the while focusing on what must be done to secure them.

Chapter Five — Crystal

"I need to get out of here!" I don't care that I'm raising my voice at this point. I've been held here like a prisoner since that giant, overbearing beast of a man left me here. Who goes from saving a person to holding the person prisoner? I don't know how long I've been here, but I could swear it's been days. The only thing that gives me an inkling of the time that's passed are the tiny windows in the room. The switch between day and night has given me the reality that I've been here too long. I need to be out of here.

"If you think I have a family who will pay ransom, you're mistaken!" I yell at the top of my voice before banging the large door with my fist. A sharp pain shoots through my hand as soon as it connects.

"Dammit!" I grimace in pain as I hold my hand to my chest and moved backward from the door. My eyes start to water . . . from the pain or maybe just being stuck here. I don't know.

"Please, let me go. I have a life," I plead, even knowing that no one can hear me. That ruthless idiot hasn't been back in the room since he left me here. I've had to deal with that stoic Hannah who only shows up to bring me herbs and different kinds of vegetable soups. I *think* they're vegetables anyway. I've never tasted anything like them in my life. I hate to admit it, but they taste better than any soup I've eaten in my whole life.

There's a room where I can bathe and more nightgowns are left for me to change into, but otherwise, I'm just here. In this room with the half-inflated floor. Waiting for . . . oh, who knows what I'm waiting for?

Dejected, I walk back from the door until I fall on the bed, a beaten down breath escaping me. I angrily wipe my tears with the back of my hand, hating myself. I hate my situation, my life, and everything, including that handsome stranger. I don't know why on earth he has been on my mind. The restlessness I've felt over the past few days is unexplainable.

"I just want to leave," I mutter before caressing my strained wrist. I still don't understand why I'm still being held here. My hand instinctively moves to my injured neck. It's completely healed and free of the scar. Goodness knows what's in those herbs Hannah always brings. It did a good job, I have to admit. However, the healed wound further proves that I've been here for too long.

I think about the fact that no one back home is looking for me. Maybe someone might miss me at work, but they'll probably all come to the conclusion that I've just quit without saying anything and go back to their own lives. I didn't have anyone who might care enough to organize a search party on my behalf. I'm alone, which means it's on me to find a way out of this place.

Aside from the restrictions inside this room, I haven't been treated like a prisoner. I dread what might happen once they know I'm a bad investment as I'm not exactly rich and no one cares enough for me to put up money for my release. If only Hannah wasn't so tight-lipped, perhaps I could have negotiated with her. I don't have much, but I've got some money in my savings. I'd give it all up if it meant my freedom.

The locks on the door turn. I sit up, looking at the door anxiously. Maybe I can run . . . or fight my way out this time. I just have to get past whoever's coming in.

I hop off the bed as the door opens and prepare myself for a fight. I take a few steps toward the door, but I'm stopped short when, instead of Hannah, a beautiful girl walks in.

She has pale skin and dark hair and she's waifishly thin. She's got big, childlike blue eyes and a pouty mouth, making her look no older than a teenager at best. Over her thin frame, she's wearing a white dress and sandals. I wondered if she was also a prisoner here.

"Hello," she says in a soft voice. Goodness, she sounds like a child too. Her voice is soft and high pitched, like a silver bell. My heart clenches as I imagine the horror she must have faced when they brought her here.

"Hi," I reply. As she walks in, it occurs to me that she can't be a prisoner at all if she could unlock my door. Oh . . . maybe she's my ticket out of here.

"Did you come to save me?" I quickly ask, hoping beyond hope. The girl's eyes widen further, and I watch her lips slightly part.

"Save you?" She asks it like the words are new to her, sounding out every syllable.

"Yes, isn't that why you came?"

"N-no. You were screaming so much and . . . I asked Mother if I could check in with you." Nothing she's saying makes sense.

"Your mother? Who . . .?" I trail off as everything starts clicking into place.

"Your mother is Hannah," I say. Of course. Why else would she be here?

"Yes." She smiles as she nods her head. I stare at her in amazement. How can someone who looks so innocent be a part of this evil plan? Maybe she's not in on this.

"My name is Leslie. My mother is the head of the healing clan," she says, and I burst into laughter.

"Clan? Are we in the Middle Ages?"

"Middle... ages? No, we are in Clarion," she responds with a puzzled look.

"Right. Clarion."

"Yes," Leslie replies.

This city or country I'm in that I've never heard of. Maybe I can get some solid information from her. "What country is Clarion in? What continent?"

"Country?"

"You see, I'm from America. I need to know how far I am from home. I don't belong here. I need to leave and find help," I explain.

"Help? We are helping you already," she says, and I scoff. I can't tell if she's just clueless or if she's like her mother and that giant.

"You call this help? I'm sorry, but where I come from, holding a person prisoner isn't the definition of helping them," I state.

"Prisoner? Oh, no. You aren't a prisoner. The dungeons are in the palace, that's where prisoners are held," Leslie says, her childlike eyes like saucers.

"Palace, dungeons? What on earth is going on here? Is this some joke? Are you all trying to drive me crazy?" I snap irritatedly. This Leslie might look sweet and innocent, but she's clearly trying to drive me crazy like the others with this weird narrative they've all concocted. These must be really big fans of fantasy novels.

"Clarion isn't a joke." She raises her voice a little, her delicate eyebrows furrowing. "It is the most beautiful dwelling for supernaturals."

I scoff. "Supernaturals? What the hell does that even mean?"

She just glares at me. It's like I've suddenly started speaking another language.

"Listen, I don't care about all of this anymore. I just want to go home. Will you help me or not?" I give her a pleading look.

"Only the Alpha King decides who can enter and leave Clarion," she says. "I could never—"

"Alpha King again," I gripe, turning away from her and running my hand through my hair frustratedly. It's like we're talking in circles. "Okay, just tell that oaf that I don't care how he runs things here. He can't keep me here against my will. It's not legal. I don't care what he says." She takes a few steps back as if I'm going to hit her. I take a breath, remembering myself.

"Look, I need to leave."

She shakes her head briskly. "Do not speak about the Alpha King with disrespect," Leslie counters, her silver-bell voice deepening. "You should be honored that Alpha King brought you here. No human has ever stepped foot into Clarion. You have been blessed with a great honor." She stands there with her head held high like she just gave me some grand speech on a mountaintop. All I can do is shake my head. *Just great; I'm in an insane asylum.*

"No human? What about you? You look pretty human to me."

"I'm not human. I'm a Mage," Leslie says defiantly. She stands a little straighter as she says this with some pride. I just glare, an eyebrow raised. *Is this girl for real?*

"My clan's duty is to help Clarion grow and create medicines that heal diseases and to use our spells for the good of all who live here." She rattles all that off like she's been trained to say it. I can't even fathom what she's talking about.

"Spells?" I'm bewildered by her words.

She pauses, reading my face carefully. "I suppose all of this *is* hard for you to understand. The human world is very different from ours. You've probably never even seen magic before."

She seems to be thinking for a moment. Then she says, "Why don't you come with me? I can show you better than I could ever explain it." She walks to the door, opening it. She looks back at me and I'm just looking at her in shock. *Is this a trick?* "Come on. But stay close. I wouldn't want you to get lost."

I walk over to her and the two of us walk out of the room together. Maybe if I'd poked fun at Hannah instead, I might've gotten this tour sooner. It occurs to me that I could just run. She was so much smaller than me. I could push her over and make a run for it, but as we stepped out into the hallway, I'm flabbergasted. The room I was in was all stone like a cave opening more than a room. This hallway was made from cool white and beige marble with intricate carvings along the moldings.

I'm just standing here looking up at it, trying to process how we're now standing in a manmade structure when we were just in a cave a moment ago.

"Clarion," Leslie says as we start walking, "is a safe haven for my people and me. Historically, we've been called many different names by humans. Shapeshifters, for example."

"Shapeshifters? Like werewolves?"

She nods. "Yes, I suppose so."

We turn a corner into the next hallway. The marble floors are covered in beautiful flower patterns. I look down at them, marveling at how they look like colorful flowers pressed under glass. I swear I can even smell their sweet, floral scent.

It's like we've just stepped into a Victorian-era mansion. The flowers run up the walls, encircling glowing sconces in the shape of foxgloves.

Leslie taps her fingers toward one of the lamps, and they all start glowing in multiple colors.

"How did you do that?" I ask, my eyes wide, taking in all the colors.

"It's part of my powers," she says with a little laugh. "According to my mother, I liked playing with lights as a child. It's a gift from the Moon Goddess."

Moon Goddess . . . right. *As logical an explanation as any,* I suppose.

"Let me show you something." Leslie grabs my hand and pulls me back around the corner to the first hallway.

"You have to be as quiet as possible," she whispers. "My people have very sharp hearing." I let her pull me along even though none of this seems real. There has to be some explanation for it all.

We run along the hallway until we reach a wall. She doesn't slow down and I grab at her hand frantically and try to dig my heels in. She's still dragging me. This girl is remarkably strong. "Whoa! Hold on!"

Just like that, we phase right through a wall. I flinch, expecting to slam right into it, but when I see that we're standing on the other side a second later, I relax, looking around in shock.

"Oh my goodness," I gasp in amazement. "How did you do that?"

"Shhh," Leslie warns, placing her fingers on her lips to silence me. I takes a few seconds before my eyes settle on our surroundings. I realize we're standing in a beautiful garden. The path that we're standing on is covered in soft green moss and there are rows and rows of different flowers, herbs and strange-looking vegetables.

There's also no sound here. I feel like we're standing in a void.

Leslie walks softly along the path and I follow her. As we move off the path, we're keeping right behind the various flower beds. I don't say a word and I try to walk as softly as she is, keeping to my word to be quiet. My hand brushes against some of the tops of the flowers, they seem to bend to me as I move. Leslie looks back and even pauses curiously, as if this is something new. She doesn't say anything, though, and we keep going.

We come to an arch of flowery vines. Leslie parts it slightly, revealing a clearing ahead of us. Hannah and two other cloaked figures stand around a purple flame, their eyes closed and their hands out around it. As we watch, the flame forms into a ball, floating up and above their heads.

I have to keep my hand over my mouth to keep from saying anything. I can't explain how they're doing this.

"Come," Leslie mouths before leading me away and towards another part of the garden. Soon, we are among a maze of beautiful red and gold flowers, carefully walking on a thin path separating them. We move until we stop in front of another flowery entrance of vines. This time, she leads me in and we're immediately surrounded by tiny blinking lights. Fireflies hovering over us and a sea of delicate white lilies. The lights move slowly away from me in a cloud as if tentatively checking me out.

"Hello, little ones," Leslie says, letting them alight on her extended hands. "This is my friend . . ." She looks over at me expectantly.

"Crystal," I say.

"Crystal," she repeats with a smile. "She means you no harm. She's our guest here."

To my surprise, as soon as Leslie says that, a thick cloud of fireflies rush out of hiding and swarm us. I start, moving back and yelping out in surprise.

"Hey, hey," says Leslie, taking me by the arm. "They're not going to hurt you."

We stand there, perfectly still, as the fireflies hover over us and a few get close enough for me to get a good look at them. I see little bodies with tiny arms and legs and wings as thin as gossamer.

"Shut the front door," I whisper. The tiny humans giggled.

"Who . . . what are they . . .?" I trail off until I notice the feel of little hands all over my back.

"They can hear you, you know," Leslie says brightly. "You can speak to them directly."

I look at all these tiny faces and I say, tentatively. "H-hi."

One of them flies forward and says, "Hello. My name is Nigel. It is a pleasure to meet you, Crystal."

"Wow, this is real," I whisper.

"As real as you or me," Leslie replies.

"These are the precious ones of Clarion. You would call them—"

"Fairies," I finish. *Real live fairies.* I can't believe what I am seeing.

"Welcome to Clarion," Leslie says.

I reach out to one of them and my hand . . . looks strange all of a sudden. As if it's covered in a golden glow. It looks like a trick of light . . . but no . . . the fairies seem to see it too. They swirl around my hand, looking at it and whispering to one another.

"How are you doing that?" Leslie asks.

I open my mouth to speak, but I have nothing to say. I don't know how this is happening. Then, just as quickly and as strangely as it appeared, the glow fades away. I lower my hand, rubbing it against my dress. It feels a little tingly still.

The fairies start to move away, the cloud of them thinning out. I look over at Leslie and her smile's gone. She's starting to look back behind us.

"Is there a problem?" I ask her.

She remains silent for a moment. Then she winces and looks up at me sheepishly. "My mother has found out we are here. She has asked us to go to the palace. Immediately."

"The palace?" Leslie nods solemnly. She looks like a child who just got caught with her hand in the cookie jar. "I don't suppose your mother's very pleased with you right now."

Leslie shakes her head. "Only Mages are allowed in the sacred coven. Come on. We should make haste."

"How do you know she's found out?" I ask her as she takes my hand and pulls me back to the wall.

"My mother is a Mage," she says simply. I guess I'll have to accept that as her answer.

We walk through the wall once more.

"You said no human has been here before? Why is that?" I ask as we walk down the hallway.

"Many years ago," she says, "humans hunted us down when our existence was discovered. We were whittled down to only a few when we found this place. The elders fortified it with magic and built it up so that many supernaturals could come here as a refuge. Just like that, Clarion was born, and we got the chance to live freely again. This place is hidden away from humans because of that history."

That's fair, I guess. Hiding away from those who've hunted you seems like a logical thing.

I'm about to ask her more when two huge men step into the hallway. They're in metal armor with faces like stone statues. We stop, frozen to the floor as fear trickles down my spine. They march towards us, their eyes burning holes into our faces.

I knew I should have run when I had the chance.

Chapter Six — Crystal

"Royal Warriors," Leslie mutters beside me as she bows her head. That does not sound good...

"Fair morning, daughter of the House of Mages," the one standing in front says, returning her gesture with his own curt bow. For a moment, I think by his show of mutual respect to Leslie, there's nothing to fear here. Then he turns his hard glare on me. I take an involuntary step back.

"Madame Crystal," he says. I mindlessly nod.

"The Alpha King has requested you be brought to the palace immediately." I look over at Leslie, who just stares back at me, her eyebrows raised. There's a part of me that's sparked a little bit of anger at being given a "request" that sounds more like a command, but my fear is still holding tight to me.

Still, I don't really take kindly to all this. I fold my arms and say, "I'm not going anywhere. If his 'majesty' wants to see me, tell him to get off his rich behind and come here."

As soon as the words leave my mouth, Leslie gasps in shock and her already too large eyes widen. The guards behind the one in the front all exchange glances behind him . . . but the main one hasn't taken his eyes off me. I'm terrified . . . but I'm holding my ground. I've had about enough disrespect to last me a lifetime.

"Crystal," Leslie whispers, "The *king* is requesting your presence. Not some overeager suitor." She turns to the guards and plasters a smile on her face. "Forgive her, good sirs. She's not from Clarion. She has no inkling of our ways and customs. We will prepare her for travel right away."

I look at Leslie and she gives me a silent look of warning, pursing her lips and raising her eyebrows.

"Preparation is not necessary," the first Warrior says. "Her presence is required before the sun reaches its zenith."

I look from the Royal Warrior to Leslie. This was happening all right. If they had to pick me up and carry me out, it was happening. I swallow hard.

"Okay, but . . . she comes with me," I tell them, nodding over at Leslie.

"Um . . .," Leslie starts. "That's not exactly appropriate. He did not call for me."

"I only feel safe around you," I say to her. "And I'm not going with these men if you're not with me."

"This is absurd," one of the men in the back mutters. The one in the forefront throws him a sharp look, silencing him.

"It's fine," he says. "But we must leave now."

He takes my arm and pulls me forward. Leslie comes running up next to me, and we all walk down the hallway. She gives me a worried look, but I mouth the words, *"Thank you,"* and she seems to relax a little. I don't know what I've just got her into, but at least I'll have an ally when we meet the king.

We walk through several different turns before we finally arrive at a large circular door leading to the outside. The first warrior waves his hand over the door and it slowly rolls out of the way to allow us through.

The bright sun blinds me for a moment as we walk outside and the cool air shocks my skin, giving me goose bumps. How long has it been since I've been cooped up in this place anyway? I feel like I'm walking outside for the first time in my entire life. After a few steps, the warm air sweeps in and I feel a little burst of energy. The day seems to be filling my body with a tingling sensation running up and down my arms and shoulders. I feel like I can fly . . .

The sweet scent of flowers greets us as we move through another beautiful garden. As we walk along the path, we pass a fountain . . . golden bowls with flower patterns on the rims, one on top of the other with water flowing down them . . .

It's . . . it's so beautiful here. Leslie and the men we're walking with don't seem fazed by it at all. I guess when beauty is your home, you reach a point where it's as normal as any city street in the world I left behind. This place should be some fancy flower museum. Beautiful just doesn't do it enough justice.

We walk away from the garden and enter what seems like a small town. We pass by houses that look like they're made of gingerbread brick with shiny, colorful roofs as we walk the streets. The stone walk under our feet looks like they've been cleaned to a high shine. I'll bet I can see my reflection in each stone.

I'm so lost in the strange, fairy tale-like structures that I don't notice the stares right away. At first, I see one woman stop and watch us pass . . . then another . . . then children stop playing just to look at us as we walk. Do Royal Warriors not walk the streets that often? Maybe seeing them escort people is a sign of trouble. It certainly feels like it.

I feel Leslie take my hand and squeeze it a little. I guess she senses my apprehension.

"Don't be scared," she says with a small smile. "They're just curious about you. No one will harm you here."

My stomach tightens. I didn't think anyone was going to harm me at all . . . but now that she's mentioned it, it makes me worry a little.

"Besides, you have the protection of the Alpha King," Leslie adds.

"That's a strange title," I say to her. "Why is he called an 'Alpha' King? Are there Beta and Gamma Kings around here?"

I didn't exactly mean that as a joke, but I see some of the people turn and grimace as soon as I say that. I wasn't speaking loudly. Did they hear me?

"Careful," says Leslie, "Some Mages have very sensitive hearing. You don't want to show disrespect to the king here."

I swallow. She didn't answer my question, and I didn't mean to offend anyone. I try again. "I didn't mean any disrespect," I say to her. "I'm just . . . curious, that's all."

She sighs and says, "His title is indicative of his place in our world. There are other kings, leaders, and members of other Royal Houses. He rules over them all. He is the Alpha."

I nod. "Must be a tough job to be born into."

"He wasn't exactly born into it. He was chosen by the Moon Goddess," she says. "She is who we worship in Clarion primarily and it is up to her who should rule over us all."

I think back to school and all the lessons about different Monarchies where kings were selected because of divine belief. Some of those kinds were thought of as Gods themselves. I wonder if that's how they think of this Alpha King.

"Do you worship him as well?" I ask her and she smiles good-naturedly.

"No, of course not. There is only one Moon Goddess. We all serve her will. All of us. Even the Alpha King."

Fascinating. Very fascinating indeed. The intellectual in me wants to know more, but as we turn a corner, the stone road ends and we come to a long, green path leading up to what looks like a walled city of lush green. Hills rise and fall for the better part of a mile, leading to a circle of stone statues, all of different animals from what I can see. And looming over it all is a great white palace with high windows and golden trim along the edges. It shines in the sunlight like a beacon.

"What is this place?" I ask in amazement.

"This is our destination," says Leslie. "The Royal Home. It's where the Alpha King lives."

"Wow," I whisper. I feel Leslie's hand tighten around mine.

"Hold on," she says.

Confused, I look over at her as the first warrior says to no one in particular, "We have arrived. Madame Crystal is with us. We respectfully request entry."

Before I can ask who he's talking to, the air changes around us. It's stinging and electric. I feel my hair standing on end. I take a breath and in the blink of an eye, we're no longer standing at the edge of the green path.

We stand in the front courtyard of the grand palace. I jump as I look around us, the sudden scenery change shocking me into stunned silence. We are standing in the center of a circular stone mosaic spanning outward to four statues around us—a lion, a bear, a tiger, and a wolf. All reared up on their hind legs, roaring as if about to go into battle.

Before us, the palace stands. Large wooden doors open and several more of these Royal Warriors stepping out. They put their fists to their chests to greet us. Our escorts say nothing as they lead us up the stairs and through the grand doors into the palace.

"Holy shit," I whisper, looking around at the marble floors and impossibly high ceilings. The first hall has white spiral pillars with gold trim leading up to a ceiling that has to be at least a couple of stories high. Way above us is a crystal . . . or maybe even a diamond chandelier twinkling from the sunlight coming in through the high open windows. This place . . . this place is magnificent.

Leslie giggles beside me, clearly at my reaction.

"The Alpha King's dwelling is beautiful, isn't it?" she says.

"At least. I don't think I've ever seen anything as beautiful in my life."

"And just think. This is just the foyer."

Our conversation is interrupted as large wooden doors open on the far side of the hall. A man with dark hair and equally dark eyes walks out. He's not a guard, but he's clearly someone of some battle importance, judging by the leather vest and sash he has on. He walks right up to the head warrior and nods. "Thank you. You may go."

They all turn obediently and leave the room, leaving Leslie and me standing there. The man looks at us both, then frowns when his eyes settle on Leslie.

"Leslie," he says, "did His Majesty request you as well?"

Leslie looks tentatively at me. "I beg your pardon, Sir Dylan, but Madame Crystal felt that she needed me for moral support."

He scoffs. "We'll see how much good that will do you."

He turns and I look at Leslie, a little offended. She has nothing to say to that.

We follow him to the door he just came out of. The room looks like a great meeting room of some sort. Large high windows with paintings on the adjoining walls. Each painting is of a different animal in battle. Wolves, bears, lions . . . all alpha predators. I guess that goes along with the whole "alpha" thing. Among the animal paintings is a painting of a man in royal garb. Another king, perhaps?

In the center of the room is a long table with at least a dozen chairs along the sides of it. "Dylan" walks away from us and to the head of the table where the Alpha King sits.

My heart races the second his dark eyes settle on me. The harsh yet simultaneously insanely handsome bastard who greeted me during my first waking moments here. He looks at me, then his eyes move to Leslie and suddenly, I feel like we're in the crosshairs of a gun.

"I don't believe I called for you, Leslie," he says casually. "Since when do you dare appear before me without requesting an audience?"

I see Leslie's face turn beet red, and I say quickly, "I asked her to come with me." I won't allow her to take the blame on my behalf. "I didn't feel safe coming alone."

"And you think this little girl can protect you from me?" he asked, lifting a single eyebrow. That feeling of fear and arousal courses through me again. I clench my jaw and push it back down to my shoes.

"Why have you called me here?" I ask. I inwardly applaud myself for keeping a brave front despite melting under his scrutinizing gaze. His eyes drift down, looking at my body through the thin nightgown. My cheeks become heated as his eyes land on my breasts and my body reacts to him as if he'd just touched me, my nipples hardening, begging for his attention.

"Leave us alone," he says, his gruff voice reverberating throughout the room and startling me. Dylan immediately walks away from his side of the door, and Leslie steps away to follow him. I grab her by the arm.

"Please. Don't go." I give her a pleading look. She touches my hand and smiles at me softly.

"I have to," she says, "but don't worry. I'll be right outside this door." She pulls her arm out of my grip and walks out with Dylan. I start to shake a little as the door shuts behind them.

Slowly, I turn my head toward the end of the long table where he's sitting, watching me. I'm shaking like a leaf under his eyes, fear and excitement coursing through me.

"Come here," he commands. An urgency to obey him washes over me, but I keep my feet firmly planted.

"I'd rather stand, thank you."

I realize my mistake seconds after the words leave my lips. A low rumble fills the room, like a lion's growl, vibrating all around me. I take a step back as I realize the sound is coming from him. I struggle to stay standing as the frantic beating of my heart against my chest threatens to make me collapse before his hard glare.

The growl dies down and he says in a stern voice, "I will not repeat myself. Do as you are told or face the consequences."

Madly, I start thinking of all the ways he might make me face a consequence, every thought dirtier than the last. I do my best to push the thoughts away, then I move towards him, giving in to his will. With each step I take, my body shakes with fear and utter desire for him. It's maddening that I feel this way. I've never wanted to be ravaged so badly in my life.

I stop when I'm a few inches away and I'm pulled into the gold in his eyes. He stands, towering over me. I'm lost in his shadow.

"Closer," he says, his voice like a low purr. I can't deny him. I close the gap between us; his sweet, musky scent encircles me, sending a bolt of arousal through my body.

What is going on with me? I can't explain this feeling . . . this need to be with him. I've never felt like this with anyone. Why do I want this so desperately?

His nostrils flare as he breathes me in. He reaches up and touches my face; his hand feels electric against my skin. I feel his other hand wrap its way around my waist, pulling me to him. He brings his face down to mine, his mouth grazing my lips . . . taunting me.

"S-stop," I stammer. To my surprise, he does. We stand there for an eternity, his breath with mine. Everything inside me is on fire as I long for his kiss . . .

"But you don't want me to stop . . . do you?" he says, his voice like a whisper in the darkness. I shake my head and it feels more involuntary than anything else.

His lips meet mine and electricity sparks between us. My hands move up to his chest, feeling his solid pecs through his clothing. I grab the fabric, the want to tear it off him, to nuzzle my face into his bare skin, is so intense. It's overpowering me.

I feel his teeth graze my lips, piercing the skin as he bites down. Soon, my tongue meets with his between the metallic taste of my own blood. He growls and I feel claws digging into my side, his raging hard-on pressed against my leg . . .

He pulls away suddenly and it's like the air has been taken from me. I stumble back, bracing myself against the table. He leans against his chair, turning away from me completely. I just stand there struggling for breath, confused as to what's just happened.

It was wonderful and frightening . . . and it felt like neither of us could control it. I don't know why he's called me here . . . but I know it wasn't for this.

"Go," he growls without looking at me. I stand there in my confusion and fear, unwilling to leave his side.

"I said LEAVE!" he bellows. I jump back and my legs are suddenly moving away from him. I turn around and rush to the doors, tears burning my eyes.

As I rush out of the room, I run right into Leslie, who stops me, grabbing me by the arms. "Crystal? What's happened? Are you all right?"

I don't know what to say. I feel tears rolling down my face and my lip is throbbing. I don't know what just happened. I can't . . . I can't . . .

Sobs come out of me and she pulls me to her, hugging me as I weep into her shoulder. I hear footsteps behind us. "Is she all right?" Dylan asks.

God, I'm causing a scene. I swallow my sobs and wipe at my face, pulling myself together as I step back from Leslie's arms. "I'm fine," I say without looking at him. "Can we please be escorted out of here?"

"I'm sorry, but I have orders to keep you here—"

"What?" I balk. "No, I . . . I can't stay here."

"You have to," said Dylan. "Leslie, you may stay with her if you like."

She nods. "That will be fine. Show us where you would like us to be, then."

Dylan nods and waves for more of those Royal Warriors to come. One of them leads us to the large staircase nearby. As we walk away, I look back at the door to the meeting room, the remnants of whatever that was still stirring within me.

Chapter Seven — Leon

That did not go as planned.

I called for her so that I could ascertain whether or not she was a spy sent by Raphael. Dylan's suggestion had been turning in my mind somewhere beyond my more carnal thoughts surrounding her. I've been trying to focus on the task at hand—protecting my kingdom.

And the second I'm alone with her, it all falls apart. As much as I'd like to deny that this human is somehow fated to be my mate... I guess I can't dismiss it entirely anymore.

The door opens and I realize I've been leaning against this chair for... who knows how long. I turn to see that it's Dylan. He stands at the threshold, eyes widened.

"... Sire?"

"What is it?"

He pauses, trying to silently evaluate my present condition. I huff. "I'm fine, Dylan. Why are you here?"

"Madame Crystal is under guard, as you have requested."

"Good." I look over at him and he's still staring. "What?"

"You're sweating, my lord."

I touch my forehead and come away with a thin sheen of sweat on my hand. Dammit. I take a handkerchief out of my pocket and wipe my forehead. "Is there anything else, or are you just here to gawk?"

He doesn't speak for a long moment, then says, "I realize that you do not wish to divert your attention from finding your brother, but . . . I would be remiss if I didn't tell you that Natasha has returned."

Natasha. My dearest Jessica's closest friend. She's been buzzing around court since her death, trying to endear herself to me under the guise of mourning. Once upon a time, I was pleased to have her nearby. When I was away with my duties, she was there to comfort Jessica in my absence. Jessica was looking forward to having her as her second once we were mated.

But friendships mean nothing in the world of royal ambition. Jessica wasn't gone a week before I found her naked in my bed one night after coming back from a hunt.

Since then, I've kept her at arm's length. When she decided to leave for a little reprieve, I was relieved. I won't lie. I was kind of hoping she wouldn't return.

"She has asked for an audience with you," Dylan continues when I don't respond. "She has brought word from the Fairy kingdom that may be of interest."

"If it is not about Raphael, I don't care."

"I wouldn't bother you if it wasn't about him," he said with a raised eyebrow.

I don't want to see her. Not after what she tried. Still . . . I need to find my brother before he wreaks more havoc on our world. I nod and Dylan steps back and through the door. The door opens again and Natasha appears.

She looks refreshed, her skin tan from the sun and her blue eyes sparkling. Her dark hair is pulled back conservatively, a change from the normal crown of waves cascading down her back as she usually likes to wear it. She's a little thinner than she was when she left, but her curves are still ample despite her athletic frame. She is still wearing her traveling cloak over her leather bodice and pants. I imagine she came directly in from the road.

She bows before me. "My King."

"Rise," I tell her. "You bring news of my brother?"

She smiles slowly at me, blood-red lips appearing more like a wound than an invitation. "No kind words for me, my lord? After all I've been to your family?"

I suppress an annoyed growl and sigh. "I would rather our relationship remain strictly professional, Natasha. You are a member of my court. Nothing more."

Her smile fades a little as she steps forward. "I see. Are you prepared for the Blood Moon? It is almost upon us, you know."

I sigh. She's getting at the one night in the year where I am compelled to find my mate somewhere in Clarion. Every year since the loss of Jessica, I have cloistered myself, too pained to allow my beasts to go roaming the land in search of someone who does not exist. I glare at her. "Why would that concern me. The time for me to have a mate has passed."

She shrugs. "The Moon Goddess could grant you another chance. Jessica's loss was tragedy enough for her to grant you a boon."

"She has not and will not, so stop fishing and get on with why you are here."

She stiffens, then says, "Well, Lady Alessandra sends her regards, and her regrets that she could not attend Jessica's burial. She hopes that you are faring well."

I nod and wave the pleasantries away. "Yes, yes. What about Raphael?"

"She has received word of the Rogues along the borders of the Fae territory. She is considering calling her subjects here in the Royal Quarter back home for their safety."

I frown. Odd. Any kind of decision of that nature, I would have heard something about from the Elders. "Why is this the first that I'm hearing about this?"

Natasha shrugs and walks over to the closest chair to me and sits. "It was a casual conversation, not a declaration," she says. "Over tea. But I thought that it was important to share her thoughts with you . . . just in case it reaches you through the proper channels. Is everything all right, my King?"

I tilt my head at her. Her eyes are scanning my face carefully. "Yes, of course. Why do you ask?"

"You appear . . . different somehow."

I casually walk around my chair and stand on the other side to give us some distance. "I was interrogating a human that Raphael attacked. I think she may be a spy."

She says nothing, staring at me with her mouth open a little. Finally, she says, "You seem flustered. Did she give you a hard time?"

"No. Of course not," I say with annoyance. "She's just a human, after all."

She nodded. "So, I take it you got nothing from her and you've released her back into the wild as you should?"

"She is staying here with me until I get all I need from her."

Natasha's face flushes. "I see. I beg your pardon, My lord, but . . . that is very unorthodox having a human here in Clarion. Especially if you suspect she is a spy."

"Are you questioning my motives?"

"No, of course not. But . . . well, don't you think it would be more prudent to return her to her world where she belongs? Where she may be . . . safer?"

I narrow my eyes at her. "I believe I already have a second and advisors," I growl at her. "And the position of Queen is permanently vacant, so why are you giving me unsolicited advise."

Her face goes beet red and her eyes widen. "I . . . I'm sorry, my lord, I just meant—"

"You are speaking out of turn . . . and you are dismissed from my presence."

She stands, her bottom lip quivering. Then she bows her head and steps back. "As you wish, Alpha King." She turns and leaves the room. Good. I don't have time for her games.

After she leaves, I take a deep breath to calm my animal sides. They rage inside me, angry at Natasha for insinuating herself, angry at Raphael for getting away...

And something else. Something more intense swirling around inside of me. The second I think of Crystal, the feeling intensifies. She's not even in the room and I can feel her through the walls.

I want to mate with her. Everything inside me wants it more than I can bear. She cannot be here. Not this close to me. Not right now.

I mind-link with Dylan. *"Send Crystal back to the Mages."*

There's nothing at first; then, *"Are you certain? It might be good to have her nearby—"*

"You heard what I said."

"Yes, my lord."

I sigh and sit down in my chair. The sooner she leaves, the more I can focus. I will need to send Warriors to Alessandra's borders to protect her lands. I may even go myself to speak with her. The Faelands are on the edge of Clarion, much farther away than the borders to the human realm. It would take me a few days travel. I don't know how wise it would be to leave this place... especially since I still don't know exactly what Crystal is.

I will have to trust that my people will protect her in my absence. I must prepare to go. It's for our own safety.

"Dylan?" I mind-link.

"Yes, my lord?"

"Once she is secured, come back here and prepare a small party for me. We will be traveling to the Faelands. Rogues have been seen along their borders."

Another pause, then, *"Natasha told you that, my King?"*

"That was her message to me, yes. Is that a problem?"

"No, of course not. I will inform you of my return."

I sit back in my chair and close my eyes, taking deep breaths to chase away the memory of her scent . . . her touch . . . her taste . . . The more I think of her, the more my mind wanders. Imagining her with her legs wrapped around me and me deep inside of her as she digs her nails into my back—

I open my eyes. My claws are out, tearing into the wood of the arms of my chair. Yes, I must be away from her. I don't know that I can control myself around her for much longer . . . and the last thing I need is a distraction.

Chapter Eight — Crystal

"What is this part called?" I ask as we stop in front of a creek.

"It's called the Dexter Forest. I used to play here a lot when I was a child," Leslie explains, beaming with pride. I glance around curiously and I have to admit it's a beautiful place . . . just like the rest of Clarion. It's all just a big, gilded, mazelike cage.

It's been a few days since he sent me back among the Mages. Leslie has been trying to keep my mind occupied with walks around the wooded area and gardens all around my prison, but it's not helping. No one has said anything about me going back home. I don't know if I'll ever be released. Hell, I don't even know why I'm here.

What's more? I don't think that I'm welcome here at all. All the Mages avoid me entirely with the exception of Leslie and her mother, Hannah ... and I'm pretty sure Hannah hates my guts. She takes care of my needs, food, clothing, whatever. But she does it with a scowl on her face and she doesn't really speak to me unless she needs something from me. Thank goodness for Leslie. She's the only thing keeping me sane here.

"Leslie, can I ask you something?"

"Sure," she says, her hand floating over a row of white and yellow flowers on the path along the creek.

"Why does your mother hate me so much?" I ask. Leslie stops and stares at me for a moment, then looks away with a sad smile.

"Once upon a time," she says, "Humans hunted Mage-kind centuries and centuries ago by your world's standards. The Alpha King of the time took up the helm to help defend them. In return, many Mages became officials amongst the Royal Warriors. My grandfather was a general, in fact. Served with Leon's father in the battles."

She sighs, her eyes looking off into the past. "War is hell ... Isn't that what humans say? It must be true. My mother had to do without both her parents during the war since they both enlisted. She lost them both to human forces."

I feel a deep sadness emanating form her. I can't imagine what it would be like to go on in the world after something like that. "How old was she?" I ask.

Leslie shrugs. "Young. She doesn't talk much about that time. Much of what I know, I've gleaned from historic teachings. My grandfather died a hero, you see. He saved the Alpha King's sister from certain death. It's even rumored that they had an affair, but I believe that was just a rumor to try and discredit his accomplishments. Mages and Shifters don't mix here, you see."

I scoff. "Sounds a little discriminatory, don't you think?"

"It is not a matter of discrimination. It's a little more complicated than that for Mages and Shifters. Other races are free to co-mingle. One of Leon's aunts was the product of a Witch/Shifter match, for example. Course, she was considered illegitimate. She was allegedly the product of an affair."

"Oh, wow," I laugh, trying to process all that she was telling me.

"That's just the gossip around town, though. Hardly a part of official history."

"Well. You certainly know a lot about Clarion history."

"It is a part of my history too. And my mother's."

Leslie's smile fades, a silence falls between us. There's nothing but the sound of the birds in the distant trees and the water lapping in the creek beside us. "The long and short of it all is that, ever since her parents died, Mother has had a bit of a grudge against humans."

"I guess I can't blame her, then," I say softly.

She pats me on the shoulder. "You shouldn't worry. Her prejudice doesn't keep her from seeing the true nature of a person. I believe she doesn't think that you're a bad human." She says this with a little smile returning to her lips.

I feel like a change of subject is in order, so I say, "Tell me about the Alpha King. You said something earlier about him being chosen by the Moon Goddess."

"Right."

"Could someone else have been chosen? I mean, the whole king thing doesn't happen by bloodline?"

"It does, but to be an Alpha King, they must have the power of the Triad and be blessed by the Moon Goddess."

I frown. "Power of the Triad," I muse. "Sounds like a video game."

She gives me a confused look but chuckles a little still. "The power of the Triad means he has the ability to shift from lion to bear to wolf. It is a *very* rare ability."

I blink dumbly at her. I don't know what she means by "shift" and "ability." "I don't think I understand."

"Shifters can only shift into one creature," she goes on. "It's considered a blessing by the Moon Goddess if you're able to shift into—"

Leslie suddenly stiffens and looks around us, her hand tightening around my arm.

"Les—"

She puts a finger to my lips, her large eyes like saucers. She takes me by the hand and drags me behind a huge rock, pulling me down to hide in its shadow.

After a few minutes, we hear the unmistakable sound of footsteps coming towards us. I glance at Leslie, who puts her finger to her lips, reiterating that I'm to remain silent. I do and we wait.

A few seconds later, a black wolf comes running into view right up to the clearing where we were both standing a moment ago. It sniffs around the grass, walking in circles as if looking for something . . . or someone. Fear seizes me as we watch it get closer to where we're hiding.

I hear Leslie breathe out a sigh of relief and she stands. "What are you doing?" I hiss. She pats me on the shoulder reassuringly.

"Lady Natasha," she says, "what brings you to the garden?"

The wolf turns to face us, then slowly I watch as the fur turns inward, exposing pale white skin. Bones crack and reform, its spine curling up and straightening as it stands on its hind legs. The legs straighten and reform, evolving into hips and thighs right before me. It doesn't take long, but a second later, we are faced with a naked woman right where a wolf once was.

I gape, trying to process what I've just seen. "Oh my God," I whisper. A *werewolf*? What kind of place is this?

"Leslie," she says with a slow smile. "I thought I smelled you out here." Her eyes turn towards me, still crouched behind the rock. "No need to bow . . . yet."

I stand and it feels more involuntary than anything else. A fear courses through me as I look at this stark-naked woman with black hair and fiery eyes. I've never been more frightened, yet Leslie doesn't even appear to be fazed.

"Do you have business here?" says Leslie and her tone is curt. It sounds strange on her. I don't think I've even heard her upset before.

Natasha looks me over, her eyes transmitting an icy-cold glare that sends goose bumps all over my body.

"So, you're Madame Crystal," she says, her voice dark like smoke. "The human that the Alpha brought to Clarion. Very interesting."

Leslie edges a little bit in front of me, drawing Natasha's eye.

"The Alpha does what he wishes without question," she says. "You still haven't told me what you're doing here."

I don't know what's happening or who this Natasha is, but I'm getting the distinct impression that there's about to me a problem between the two of them.

"The Alpha does what he wishes," Natasha repeats as she starts to circle us. "Yes, well, I wonder what is it about this human that makes him break Clarion law?"

"That's not for you to say," Leslie says. "It would be wise for you to leave us in peace."

"Would it?" Natasha cocks her head, her fangs showing. A second later, I'm pushed hard, thrown into a tree with Natasha's face inches from mine, her eyes glowing and her teeth snarling at me.

I panic and try to push her away, but her hand is around my neck and the air is being squeezed out of me.

"Natasha, stop this!" I hear Leslie yell. "Release her immediately."

"You are not worthy of him," she snarls at me. "You are a weak, useless human. You could never be his mate—"

She's yanked away from me, a glow surrounding her as she goes sailing through the air, landing on the ground a few feet away. The sudden release leaves me gasping as I fall to my knees, holding my throat.

I hear Leslie rush to my side, her hand on my shoulder.

"Are you okay?" she asks. I manage to nod in response. Leslie stands up and faces Natasha as she gets to her feet.

"She is not to be harmed under order of the Alpha King," Leslie says. "Maybe you've been away too long to realize."

Natasha's eyes are glowing like fire and she's snarling with long fangs. "You do not dictate orders to *me*," she says as a deep growl wells up from inside her. She howls, her voice taking on a multivoiced symphony of animal and human. Her body changes again, bones cracking and shifting as dark fur covers her body.

"Run," says Leslie. "I'll hold her off."

I don't have time to object because Natasha is barreling towards us. I see Leslie throw her hands forward, sending light at Natasha and pushing her backward. This time, Natasha dodges her, claws extended as she swipes across Leslie's face and sends her to the ground.

"No!" I scream. The wolf turns towards me and starts to leap, but Leslie leaps up, one side of her face bleeding from the long, deep scars she just received.

"Run! Crystal!" she screams as she holds on to Natasha.

My feet start moving before I can process what's happened. I run through the woods, my mind spinning. I need to find help. Leslie . . . oh God, Leslie!

I'm knocked down, falling forward from the weight of the wolf on my back. I hit the ground, my head slamming against a rock.

As consciousness slips away from me, I see Natasha change back into a human. She stares down at me coldly as everything goes black.

"You will *never* be his mate," she hisses before I pass out.

Chapter Nine — Leon

Word of the attack reaches me as soon as I enter Clarion. A shifter attack on one of the Mages. Hannah's daughter, Leslie, to be specific. I've wasted no time in finding Dylan, who is in the forest at the edge of the Mage Gardens, the scene of the attack. I walk into the area and I see him standing with the other Mages next to a patch of bloody leaves and bushes. He spots me almost immediately and leaves them to talk to me.

"What happened?" I ask.

"A shifter attacked Leslie and we suspect they grabbed the human."

An ice-cold wave of fear washes over me. "Crystal? She was taken?"

"According to the other Mages, the two of them went for a walk a little while ago. Leslie managed to send up an alarm before she passed out."

I take a moment and scent the air. It's thick with blood and fear . . . but also something else. A very familiar scent, in fact. I recognize it, and the second I do, I look down at Dylan, who already knows what I'm thinking.

"Natasha," I hiss and he nods.

"This holiday she's taken was clearly a ruse. She is clearly in league with Raphael."

As much as I know that it has to be her who initiated the attack, a part of me doesn't want to believe it. For everything that Natasha has been, she has never been disloyal. It has always been her misguided love for me that has kept her allegiance to my rule. Clearly, that has changed for some reason.

"She has always been loyal," I protest halfheartedly. "She knows the penalty for treason. Why would she do this?"

Dylan takes a deep breath, gearing up to express his thoughts. "Sire, if I may ask . . . were any of Raphael's forces in the Faelands?"

My stomach turns. There were not. "Lady Alessandra was surprised at my arrival," I tell Dylan. "She reported nothing of the sort."

I'm thinking back to the conversation I had with her when I arrived. The look of shock on her face as I walked into her realm. She greeted me courteously . . . but it was clear that she had no idea what prompted the visit. On the way back home, I thought that perhaps Natasha got the information wrong, even though it wasn't like her to misquote messages.

I know now that it was a well-placed ruse. She had to make sure I was away in order to launch her attack.

"The attack happened only an hour ago, by my estimation," says Dylan. "If we hurry, we may still track them."

"Then let us be on our way."

A loud growl leaves my mouth as I allow my wolf to lead me. My bear and lion are as restless as my wolf. It started a few minutes ago when a sharp pain ran through my body, signaling their need to take over. I am filled with such turmoil over this, my control starting to lose its ground with every moment I am apart from Crystal.

I don't know if I'm going mad or if Dylan was right all along. All I know is that I cannot lose Crystal. This abduction and her life being in danger has shades of the day I lost Jessica. I feel like my entire life as Alpha King was forever cursed on that day . . . and I cannot let it happen again.

I bolt through the woods, following Crystal and Natasha's scent. Dylan runs beside me, but I can see that he's struggling to keep up. We cannot stop. Even if I must leave Dylan behind.

"Sire," he mind-links with me. *"Hold on. I must catch my breath."*

I don't want to stop, but I do for him. We slow and I look at him as he nearly falls over from exhaustion. *"Are you well?"* I ask.

"I just need a moment. We've been running hard since we left the gardens."

"We cannot lose the scent," I mind-link back to him with a bit of annoyance. *"If she gets away—"*

"I will catch up." He looks up at me with his yellow wolf eyes, head hanging low and his tongue hanging out as he pants. *"Go on."*

I turn and leave him. Dylan is a better tracker than I, but he's no good to me if he passes out from exhaustion. I turn and continue following the path leading me to the both of them.

It doesn't take long before I reach the end of the trail and come to a clearing on the edge of the Clarion border. Lying in the center of the clearing is Crystal. The grass beneath her is red with her blood and from here, I can't tell if she's living or dead.

Fear fills my heart as I rush over to her, shifting back into human as I take her into my arms. "Crystal?" Her head lolls limp against me, her dark hair sticky with blood. *What have they done to you?*

"She did that to herself, you know? The head wound."

The voice shocks me into attack mode and I look up and around myself. A moment passes and a cloaked figure steps into the light. He pulls down his cloak, revealing his long dark hair and amber eyes.

"Raphael," I growl. I don't want to let Crystal go, but every animal inside me is ready to fight. Raphael just smiles at me, his eyes growing dark as he steps toward us.

"When I sent Natasha to fetch her," he says, "I gave her explicit instructions to deliver her unharmed. I suppose I should have asked her to keep her from running and tripping over a rock."

I stand, creating a barrier between him and Crystal. "This was your plan? To lure me out here and what? Challenge me for the throne? If it's a fight you're looking for—"

"You were always so quick to rush to fisticuffs," he says. "Hold your beasts back, Brother. We're not there yet."

I tilt my head at him. He stands with his hands behind his back and I sense no tension from him. He's acting like he's in total control of this situation.

"You know the Blood Moon is coming," he says with a sinister smile. "What will you do when it comes? Do you bind yourself with chains or do you search endlessly for a mate that will never come?"

He's trying to antagonize me, trying to get me to release the beasts within me so he can gain even more control over me. With a stiff lip, I glare at him in defiance. "You have committed the highest acts of treason," I say to him, "and now you wish to parlay with me? I will rip your arms off and beat you senseless with them."

I step towards him and I hear movement in the trees. The sudden smell of wolves are all around us, moving through the shadows, waiting for his command. I freeze, realizing how foolish it would be for Raphael to go anywhere alone. It's a good play. One I should have anticipated.

"This is a very interesting situation we have found ourselves in," he says. "You came here on your own. Without so much as your second at your side. For the life of a human? This would be the second time that you've come to her aid. I find that very interesting."

There is more to this than what he is saying. His random attack wasn't random at all, it seems. "You were her attacker," I say, edging toward him. "Why?"

"She's special," he says, "but that's not something that you don't know already. Why else would you come here alone?"

We're playing chess now. He starts to circle me and I keep my senses sharp, ready for any attack that he might be giving.

"I knew you would come for her. And now that you have, I finally have your undivided attention."

"You have never lost it," I growl at him.

"Well, I suppose that is true. Now, I imagine you are more willing to listen."

"Get on with it," I say. He stops in front of me, an arm's length away. I could rip his throat out with one slash of my claws.

"I want a land of my own," he says. "Somewhere in Clarion. A place that I can rule over without your intervention. A place where I can be Alpha."

I can't believe what I'm hearing. I glare at him. "You've gone insane," I say. "The whole of Clarion is ruled by me and me alone. It is ancient law—"

"It is wrong. I am the true Alpha. I was bred for it. I was born first. I was better at all my training than you. I—"

He stops himself, his claws and fangs protruding. His own animal struggling to get out.

"Just because you possess the Triad," he hisses, "does not mean you are worthy."

"It is exactly what it means, Raphael. I was chosen by the Moon Goddess and you were not. And besides, even if I were to grant you some kind of clemency, have you forgotten your crimes? All the human attacks? My mate? Our father?"

"Enough!" Raphael roars. "One way or another, I will be the Alpha King. And if you will not listen to reason, then I have no choice but to take what is rightfully mine."

He points one clawed finger at me, then backs away, a slow grin on his face. "Expect us," he says, "for I shall show you no mercy in battle."

He turned, changing into a wolf and running into the dark of the trees. I stood there, cold and angry, wanting so much to go after him. Even alone. Even with no forces at my command.

I can't leave Crystal. She's barely alive and still bleeding. She needs medical care immediately.

I lean back down to her and Dylan comes crashing through the brush, an excited look in his eyes. He shifts to human and says, "Alpha King, I smell other wolves. Are you—?"

"I'm fine," I say as I kneel down next to Crystal. Her eyes are fluttering. She will probably wake soon. "We need to get her back to the Mages."

"Are you sure you don't want anything else, Alpha King?" Hannah quietly asks. My eyes remain on my bejeweled Crystal. Two days have passed, and she has neither opened her eyes nor made any movement. It worries me despite Hannah's reassurances. As I sit next to her, all I can think about is going after Raphael and Natasha for this and making them pay. But that's not all I'm thinking about.

Raphael chose her specifically because she is "special." The way I've acted around her since her arrival, I know how special she must be . . . but how can he know it? How could he have known it before I ever knew her?

"I'm fine, Hannah," I reply. She nods silently and backs away.

"As you wish, Sire," she says as she leaves.

I focus back on Crystal, still and pristine as a statue lying in slumber. She is special . . . to me. And if there was any doubt before now as to whether or not she is fated to me, it's gone. Those moments I spent looking for her, thinking about what I might do if she were dead . . . I can't even fathom what I might do if she does not live through this.

The Moon Goddess must be really messing with me to thrust someone like this at me. I wonder what this all means. To take Jessica from me, then to present me with Crystal. I don't know whether I am cursed or blessed.

The Triad within me paces impatiently. Being so close to Crystal and being unable to exact revenge in the way of a hunt has rattled them. These last two days have been the longest two days of my life.

"Please wake up, my jewel," I whisper to her, taking her hand and kissing it. I'm thinking about the night before my first mating and finding Jessica on the floor of her room in a pool of her own blood, the life leaving her as I ran to her. It was the first in all the horrors that Raphael would wreck on us that day. Later I would find my father's body . . . and the trail of bodies from all the warriors trying to defend us.

I close my eyes and press her hand to my forehead.

"I promise to protect you from now on," I whisper. "No harm will ever befall you again."

I feel her fingers twitch against my skin and I think that I'm imagining things. I look up at her and see her eyes are still closed. I go to lower her hand and I feel her gently squeeze it.

"Crystal," I call her name, hoping she hears me. Her eyes flutter open. My joy rises inside as she turns her head to me.

Her eyes look me over as if trying to focus in. "Water," she whispers faintly. I let go of her hand and rush to the pitcher of water Hannah left on the end table near the window. I fill a cup and rush back to Crystal's side, gently helping her as she lifts her head weakly to get a sip. She drinks for a long time before pushing the cup away and lying back down.

"My head . . .," she whispers. She goes to touch the bandage on her forehead, but I stop her, pulling her hands back down gently. "What . . . what happened?"

"You were attacked," I say. "But you're safe now. You're being cared for."

She looks at me again and, perhaps for the first time since we met, she smiles gently at me. "Thank you," she whispers.

"Lie back. I'll go get Hannah." I start to stand, but she grabs my hand, holding me back.

"No, don't leave me," she whispers.

"I'm only going to find Hannah. I won't be long."

"Stay," she insists. "Please."

I sit back down, entwining her hand with mine. My connection with her is so strong now I can't stand to leave her anyway.

"Was it you that saved me?" she says, a small smile on her face. I nod. She turns her eyes away for a moment. "Of course it was. I can't go two steps without you in my way."

There's no malice in her voice. No anger. I feel nothing but a warm familiarity with her. I bring her hand to my lips and kiss it.

"You gave me quite a scare," I say to her. "We thought . . . I thought—"

"You should know by now that I'm tougher than everyone seems to think. I'll probably be up and walking around any moment."

She looks over at me, then releases my hand to brush a bit of my hair out of my eyes. She looks into my eyes and tilts her head. My heart pounds and the Triad inside me purrs at her touch.

"You need to rest," I tell her. "Even if you are a fast healer."

She nods. "Then stay with me until I fall back to sleep?"

"Of course."

She smiles and takes my hand in hers. We are here together in this place with nothing but the birds outside to cut through the warm silence between us. Before long, I'm resting my head on the bed next to her and her hand is on my head, her fingers in my hair. In this moment, I am hers and she is mine. The world, the laws, and maybe even our own minds are irrelevant. I rest my head on the bed with her and it is enough to calm the beasts inside me.

I will do anything for her. She is the one I am fated to be with.

Chapter Ten — Leon

"Alpha King?"

The sound of Dylan's voice awakens me. I open my eyes and lift my head. I'm still sitting by Crystal's bedside. My neck is sore from having fallen asleep here. I sit up and stretch my back a little, then stand and lead Dylan out of the room to speak.

"You bring news?" I ask. He nods quickly.

"We have found and captured Natasha," he says. "She awaits you for questioning."

The fire in me is relit. My Triad rumbles like the coming tremor of an earthquake. Part of my vengeance is at hand. "Take me to her."

We walk through the halls and then out of the Mage Gardens. Outside, I see Hannah and Leslie among the flowers, gathering herbs. Leslie looks as well as she always has, her wounds completely healed from the strong healing magic her mother possesses. They see me and bow immediately.

"Your Majesty," Hannah says, "how does the human fare?"

"She is healing," I say. "She opened her eyes a little while ago, but she is resting comfortably now."

Both Hannah's and Leslie's eyes widen at the news. "Well, she truly is a wonder," says Hannah. I'm not sure if she's being sarcastic or not.

"I must away for now. See that she is guarded and cared for until I return."

"Of course, Your Majesty."

I don't wait for any responses or questions. Natasha awaits us in my royal court.

When we walk into court, two of my warriors are flanking Natasha as she kneels before my throne. Her long dark hair is mussed, and she is dressed in rags. I'm told by Dylan that she was caught as a wolf, so when she shifted back to human, she remained in her naked human form all the way back to the palace. She wasn't given clothing until she was jailed.

I walk past her to my throne, glaring down at her with disdain. "Give me one reason why I shouldn't have your head."

She flinches as my voice echoes off the walls of the room. I sit down on my throne as she keeps her head down out of respect.

"Speak, treacherous woman!" I bellow. She flinches, then lifts her head. Her eyes are red and wet with tears.

"I did what I had to," she says. "You gave me no choice, my King."

My Triad rages inside me. I hold it back. "*I* gave you no choice? Care to explain yourself?"

She swallows hard, her eyes darting around the room. Perhaps to look for an escape? There is none. She knows that more than anyone.

"The woman . . .," she says. "It is rumored that you will choose her for your mate soon. You cannot. She . . . she isn't—"

"Oh, this is *rich*," I laugh. "You joined Raphael's forces because you think I am going to mate with a human? Have you completely taken leave of your senses?"

She shakes her head slowly, a lone tear rolling down her cheek. "I know that this woman is something more than human," she says.

"Do you? Is that what the rumors say?"

"They did not need to. Raphael was the one to sense it first. He was searching for her . . . became obsessed with her. I thought it would pass, but . . . but when he finally found her—"

I put my hand up to stop her as I put together the depth of her treason. "How long have you been allied with Raphael, Natasha?" She starts to breathe in shallow breaths and her eyes widen. "Answer me!"

She yelps out in surprise, new tears rolling down her face. "You . . . you rejected me," she began, choking back sobs. "You said I would never be your mate despite everything I've done for you and this court. Despite it all, you still would not accept me. I still wanted to be loyal to you, my King. You must believe me. I tried to think of you as just my Alpha King . . . but when Raphael approached me one day while I was in town . . ."

She trailed off. The Triad is in full rage. I feel my fangs itching at my gums. Dylan touches my arm and says, "It would be good for you to allow her to finish, Sire."

She shakes her head, a faint smile on her face. "He is very like you, Leon," she says softly. "In the best ways. He was kind to me and gentle . . . and he promised that I would be protected. He felt betrayed by your father. Said that he never really gave him a chance after the Moon Goddess chose you. He told me that your father turned all his attention to you after that. It was like he just threw him away in the trash. All . . . all he wanted was to have his family back. And when he realized that would never be . . ."

Something in her tone is piercing through the stone around my heart. Suddenly, I realize that Natasha's treason is not out of a lust for power. She speaks of my brother like . . . like a companion. She found the like mind of someone who had been rejected by the one person they believed in more than anything.

"I . . . I tried to heal that need in him for a family," she goes on, trying to hold back her sobs. "I thought that if I gave the love I'd saved for you to him, then maybe that would stop his bloodlust for the throne."

"I see it didn't work," I say to her, trying to remain cold. "He's still launching attacks on humans—"

She shakes her head. "No, you don't understand." She pauses, her eyes suddenly wild. It seems like she might try to flee. She closes her eyes for a moment, then continues.

"I . . . I am with child, my King," she says. "The moment he discovered that I was carrying his cub . . . he set about a plan to make you bend to his will. To preserve a place for the both of us to live in peace instead of waging war and risking his life. He very much wants to be in this child's life . . . and so do I. For that, I beg you to spare me for what I've done. For the sake of my whelp, I beg you."

I'm stunned. I just stare at her, my mind spinning as I try to decipher if she is telling the truth or not. But . . . but it makes sense. The increase in attacks were him looking for Crystal, knowing that she would attract me. What a grand scheme . . . and all for the life of his unborn cub.

"Sire," said Dylan, "perhaps you should rethink your position with Natasha. The execution of a pregnant Shifter—"

"I am aware of how it would look," I hiss at him. I can't think. My rage at my brother has become complicated and as I look down at this woman who has been drawn into his web . . . I'm left to decide the fate of not one but two. One of which is the most innocent of them all.

"Take her to the dungeons," I tell my warriors. Everyone pauses, looking at me like I've grown antlers.

"Her sentence, Alpha King?" Dylan asks.

"The dungeons," I repeat. "Until I decide what will be done with her, that is where she will be."

My Royal Warriors lift her to her feet and escort her out immediately. Once she's gone, Dylan steps in front of me.

"This woman has caused quite a bit of strife for you," he says. "Perhaps we should find out what makes her special enough to cause Raphael to use her for his schemes."

I wave him away. "This is about more than that," I say. "Raphael lost his family long before he raised his claw to our father and to Jessica . . . and now he's willing to burn all of Clarion down over it. I do not know why I feel the way I do for Crystal or why Raphael knows that I would be drawn to her . . . but that is secondary to the fact that he has nearly destroyed Natasha in that struggle."

Dylan doesn't say anything for a long moment. Finally, he breaks his silence and asks, "What's the next step, then, my lord?"

I take a deep breath, the Triad swirling around inside of me, pacing like the impatient beasts they are.

"I need to go for a run," I say. "I need to think. Watch over things here for me."

"Of course, Alpha King."

I stand and give in to the beasts inside me, leaning into my wolf form and bolting out of the room and through the palace until I'm out and in the wild again. I need to think. I need to get away for a moment and think all this out.

My brother's betrayal cannot be undone . . . but he was wronged first by my father. I feel like I've been blinded by my loss to see that it all came back around to create the monster he's become. What shall I do? How do I stop this chain of madness that has come over my bloodline?

I reach my favorite spot just beyond the palace walls. A waterfall surrounded by a lake of gold flowers. A peaceful oasis in the center of my sea of turmoil. I shift back into a human and dive into the water, letting the cool waves calm me. I can think a little clearer now. It's all become so clear to me.

I can't punish Natasha for her actions. She was misguided in her love for me and for Raphael. In her own twisted way, she was trying to protect my family as well. I cannot fault her for that.

I get out of the water and change back into a wolf, laying in the sunlight with closed eyes. I don't know yet what I will do about my brother, but I believe I'm seeing things clearly for the first time in a long time.

I'm only here for a little while before I begin to think of Crystal. She may be awake now. I should go and be by her side. I get up and start my trek to the Mage Gardens to see her once more. It's then that I pick up her scent. Distinctive in its sweetness, I stand slowly as the wolf, my eyes peering into the woods.

It's only a few moments, but she appears finally, stepping into the light slowly, her eyes large with fear. I realize that she's not looking at me as a man. She must be terrified . . . yet she doesn't run from me. She only stands cautiously away.

"Leon?" she says softly.

Chapter Eleven — Crystal

The wolf slowly turns, the body shifting from beast to human before my eyes. I watch with a mix of fear and fascination as his bone structure changes and his black fur melts back into his skin. Then he's standing before me, naked. His muscular body shines from the water he was just swimming in. My eyes drift down to his abs, then down to the massive cock swinging between his muscular thighs.

I flush and turn away from him. Intrigued and embarrassed all at once. "Sorry," I say. "I didn't realize you would be . . . naked."

My heart beats wildly as I try not to look at him. I'm amazed that he's just standing there, naked as the day he was born and we're outdoors.

"Is there a problem?" he asks me, his baritone sending tremors through my body.

"I . . . you aren't wearing any clothes."

He doesn't say anything for a moment. I dare a look at him only to see him cocking his head in curiosity at me. "Does that bother you?"

"Just not used to it," I say and realize that my voice is entirely too high. As embarrassed as I am, a part of me feels like it's on fire. I yearn to feel his touch.

As if he can read my mind, I hear his feet padding along the grass. I look up in time to see that he's walking towards me. He stops and reaches out to me, his warm hand brushing back my hair and touching the small scar on my forehead.

"Already healed," he said. "What are you doing this far from the gardens?"

A conversation to divert me from the fact that he's completely naked. Okay. I'll take it. I look up into his eyes, purposely avoiding looking down.

"I came for a walk," I whisper in return. I can feel his body heat enveloping me the way it did that first day when he called me into his palace. *Make a move,* my mind says. *He's already naked . . .*

I push the crude thought away as he smiles down at me, his eyes gentle.

"You should be resting," he says. He's right, I should be. When I woke up, he was gone from my side and I became restless. I can't explain it, but it's like my body is tuned to his presence. I want him close just like this. Sharing our space and the heat of our bodies. I guess that confused feeling made me take a walk despite Hannah's insistence that I wasn't fit for it. I feel fine, though and walking has always helped me clear my head. I wasn't expecting to see the largest wolf I'd ever seen lying in the grass. I also wasn't expecting to know without knowing that it wasn't a wolf at all. I knew him before he revealed himself to me.

"It was beautiful," I say, seemingly apropos of nothing. He stares at me in confusion.

"You . . . as a wolf. It was majestic. I've never seen anything so beautiful." What am I saying? I shouldn't be talking like this. It's like the words are just falling out of my mouth. Fortunately, Leon is still smiling. I guess I haven't completely embarrassed myself.

"Thank you," he says. "I noticed that you didn't run from me. What if it was someone else? Someone who could harm you? You should be more careful about the wolves you meet in Clarion."

I shrug. "I don't know how, but I knew it was you and I know that you promised no harm would come to me."

"Even at that," he says, his voice vibrating me to my core. "You should be more careful. I would never want to see you hurt again."

That makes me smile a little. *He . . . genuinely cares about me. How strange.* "You were with me the whole time I was unconscious . . . weren't you?"

He stiffens like I just revealed some grand secret I'm not supposed to know. He turns away from me like he's going to distance himself. I don't want that. I reach out to him, grabbing hold of his arm. My hand does nothing to cover the circumference of his bicep, but he stops just the same at my touch.

"Don't," I say. "Please."

He relaxes a little, then says, "You were under my care. I promised no harm would come to you, and yet . . ." He trails off, his face a mask of disappointment. Is this guilt? That's disappointing. I'd rather he stayed because he cared about me.

"So, it was just pity, then, that made you stay?" I ask him genuinely. He looks back at me, the most earnest I've ever seen his dark eyes.

"No," he whispers. "I stayed because . . . because I failed you. Crystal, I am inexplicably connected to you. From the first moment I saw you, I knew you . . . you were destined to be mine."

It seems to be hard for him to say. My heart feels like it's melting and alive all at once. He's speaking the words that I've always somehow known all along.

"You care about me . . . really? This is about more than just your being Alpha King and all that. You . . . care."

He takes a breath and steps back to me, towering over me, his warm, naked body calling to me again.

"You have no idea what it felt like to find you lying there, clinging to life. To know that you were so close to leaving this world and it would be my fault." He looks at me with so much pain in his face. "It felt like my world was crashing. There was no place I would rather be than by your side," he adds. "I wasn't with you out of pity or guilt, Crystal. I was with you because there was nowhere else I would rather be."

I can feel his pain, his anguish, his warmth, and love all mixed together, surrounding me, pulling me in. He leans into me and I throw my arms around his neck, pulling his mouth down to mine and breathing in his woody scent.

The sweet taste of his lips explodes in my mouth as he holds my chin, the air exploding between us. Nothing

I have imagined before this moment compares to reality. His kiss is ambrosia and mountains colliding. I'm losing all sense of reasoning as his arms move down to my waist and pull me closer, pressing me flush against his body. His massive erection is pressed against my thigh and it makes me hungry for him. I bite his lip playfully and I feel him smiling against me.

I want this so badly. I gasp softly as his mouth moves down to my neck, the sharp points of fangs sliding along my skin and sending waves of anticipation throughout my body. His hands move up to my breasts, fondling them through the thin fabric of my gown, his thumbs finding my hardening nipples.

"Yes," I whisper. "Take me."

He growls, a rumble vibrating against my skin and through my body. I'm on fire and I already feel slick between my thighs. I've never wanted anyone as badly as I do him.

He lifts his head to my mouth and kisses me deeply again. I reach down, running my fingers along his rock-hard abs and down to his waiting cock.

He pulls away, out of the kiss and grabs my hand to stop its progress. Confused, I look up at him wantonly, desperate to have him back again.

"Crystal, wait . . . we can't."

I look at him as he steps back from me. The air is suddenly so cold around me. My heart reaches out to him as he holds my hands, binding me.

"Did . . . did I do something wrong?" I ask him. He shakes his head.

"No, of course not. It's just . . . we can't continue this. There's too much at stake and . . . we just can't."

I'm so confused right now. What is he even talking about? "Leon, I want to be with you. Right here, right now. Why do you want to stop?"

He sighs and releases my hands, turning away from me entirely. He's . . . he's walking away.

"Leon!" He stops, but he doesn't look back. "You can't just walk away from me like this," I say. "Not without an explanation or something. I know you want me just as much as I do you. There's nothing holding us back except you."

He turns and looks at me. "There is much you don't know and probably shouldn't know. I've involved you too much as it is and . . . if we don't stop now, I may not be able to control myself. I can't risk that."

"You're not making any sense."

He sighs. "Please, Crystal, just know that I mean the best for you—"

I walk to him, around him, to cut off his path and look him in the eye. My excitement is turning to anger. "Don't give me that lost, brooding bullshit," I say angrily at him. "You can't string me along like this. Either you want me, or you don't. Simple as that."

"You're angry," he says.

"You're damn right I am," I mutter, glaring at him.

"Why did you bring me here?" I push. "You just said you were drawn to me from the moment you saw me. *Drawn,* dammit! And now things get a little too hot and you want to push me away! What kind of games are you playing here?"

He stares his brow furrowing and his dark gaze becoming hard and cold.

"Because you're more connected to Clarion than you can imagine," he says.

"What does that even mean? Stop with this cryptic bullshit and just tell me!"

He sighs, then says, "I believe that you are not human, Crystal. That you're something else. And that something is what has drawn danger to you."

"Danger?" I say, taking a shocked step back. "You mean, that Natasha woman? That kind of danger?"

"It's complicated. Much more complicated than I have the time or inclination to explain."

I scoff. This haughty attitude of his is getting on my nerves. "All right. I'm not human. Then what am I?"

"Honestly, I don't know . . . yet. I need to find out, though, if you are ever going to be safe."

"And what does that have to do with being with me?"

To my surprise, he smirks and says, "You ask too many questions."

"Because you don't answer enough of them," I bark back. "Jesus, Leon. Just tell me what's going on."

"I don't know it all yet. What I do know is that whatever you are puts you in danger . . . and may harm my empire if we . . . we were together." I blanch, but he continues. "I do not yet know if you are capable of help or harm. I don't even know if being with you could elevate me or destroy me . . . or perhaps nothing at all. All I do know right now is that if I let you return to your home, you will be unprotected and in grave danger."

I nod. "So, that's why I'm here, why I can't go back home."

"Yes. I brought you here on instinct, not fully understanding why you needed protection. But now I see the very real dangers that exist for you out there, and why it's necessary to keep you here."

I don't know what to do with this information. I stand there for a long moment until he says, "I must return to the castle. I have duties to attend to."

He walks around me and I turn, that annoying instinct to be with him stiffening inside me. "Wait. Take me with you."

"No."

"I don't need to be with the Mages anymore. I feel fine. There's no reason—"

"The reason is that I said no."

I cross my arms defiantly. "I'll just follow you. Do you want me to walk alone through these woods with no protection?"

He rolls his eyes. I'm annoying him, but I think maybe he's enjoying it a little.

"All right. How about I escort you back to the caves instead? You should have a once-over from Hannah before you declare yourself well."

"Okay," I say. I guess that's a reasonable compromise. I blink at him, then I chuckle. "Aren't you going to put on some clothes?"

He glances down at himself, then, "Why? It is a warm day. There's no need—"

"Oh my God. You just walk around naked here and nobody cares?"

He shrugs. "It's not a problem in Clarion like it is in the human world. Which I've always been particularly curious about if we're being honest. Why are you so ashamed of your bodies?"

I snort a laugh. "It's complicated."

We start to walk, taking the path that I'd found leading back to the gardens. I have so many questions that I doubt he can answer, but this is fine for now. I look over at him in all his nakedness, still walking with his head held high like the king that he is. It's funny, I've never called him "Sire" or "my King." Maybe I should have?

"Is something the matter?" he asks me, catching the perplexed look on my face.

"I've been calling you by your first name all this time," I say. "I'm not being disrespectful, am I? I mean . . . I guess I just didn't think much about it."

He pauses like the subject hasn't even occurred to him. "I'm fine with it, actually."

"Really?" He nods. "So, you're okay with me calling you Leon?"

He blinks. I don't think it's occurred to him that that's pretty much what I've been calling him the whole time. "You can call me Leon," he says. "I don't know how you knew my name, however. No one calls me that."

I just shrug. I don't know how I knew either. Maybe it was all a part of this inexplicable connection between us.

"I'm honored," I say with a coy smile.

Chapter Twelve — Leon

Anticipation fills me as I walk to the entrance of the Mage caves. It's been two weeks since we started afresh on a friendly note, and it's been the best time of my life.

Seeing Crystal let go around me is the most pleasurable thing. We've gone for walks in these woods nearly every day and she holds my hand freely and leans close to me, stepping into the warmth of my body. We talk endlessly about our lives and I've even shared a little bit about my world and my life.

I've not told her about the details of losing my father and Jessica or my brother's continued campaign against me. I've chosen to keep her out of those matters for now. On the other side of that, I've asked both Dylan and

Hannah to look into her and find something that gives me even a clue as to what she truly is. I don't think she knows herself . . . but it might be a good thing for the two of us if I discover the secret her body holds.

Speaking of her body . . . I'm finding it harder and harder to fight my attraction to her. My Triad paces inside me, wanting me to claim and mate with her every time we're together. Because of my animal instincts, I've had to cut my visits shorter and shorter. I don't want to lose control around her.

I don't know why this is happening and it's hard for me to believe that the Moon Goddess has given me another chance. However, the fear of the unknown restrains me. What if I claim Crystal and lose her like I lost Jessica? What if she is not as resilient as she appears and I kill her myself trying to mate with her? What if the elders do not accept her as my chosen mate? Such a thing could cause so much political turmoil, which is the last thing we need right now with Raphael still on the loose.

The thought occurs to me that I should cut my time short and leave while I can. Maybe I can miss a day with her. Maybe she wouldn't mind. Maybe—

Leslie comes walking out and the second she sees me, she bows.

"Alpha King," she says.

"Greetings, Leslie. How are you today?"

She stands, a wide smile on her cherubic face. "I'm fine, my lord. Thank you for asking. Would you like to come in?"

She steps aside so that I may pass. I wave her off. "That won't be necessary. Would you please call Crystal for me?"

"Of course, Alpha King. I'll return promptly." She turns and rushes back inside, a hint of a smile on her lips.

What am I doing? A second ago, I was about to leave and now I stand in wait for her. I've never felt so attached to a female like this, not since Jessica. Maybe . . . maybe this is meant to be more than I was hoping after all.

It feels like mere seconds before the door opens again; this time, Crystal steps out. As usual, she wears the gowns left to her by the Mages, white, thin linen that leaves very little to the imagination in this light. The urge to damn all consequences and have her is on the high side. She walks towards me with an innocent smile and I push down my carnal urges.

"Leon. It's a little late in the morning for another walk, but I'm glad you're here," she says. "I could use some time to stretch my legs."

"Actually," I say, "I'm here for another purpose."

I can sense Leslie somewhere behind her in the shadows. Listening. It's a little juvenile, but I can't complain too much. I seem to recall Jessica's friends giggling in the background when I went to visit her in the early days of our courtship.

Plus, Leslie is probably wondering what my interest is in her. I imagine everyone is.

Crystal raises her eyebrows in question. "Oh?"

"Yes, I was hoping we could share dinner at the Royal House." A slow smile appears on her face, complementing the arch in her eyebrows.

"Are you asking me out on a date?" There's a touch of a laugh on the edge of her voice. She finds this amusing.

"You can call it that," I say, matching her energy. "We've been getting along so well lately, I thought—"

"Of course, I'd love to have dinner with you," she says. Her smile is warm and inviting, and I am charmed. There's something endearing about the way she looks at me and it makes even the Triad go silent in reverence of her.

"Wonderful. Shall we go?"

She blinked, her smile dropping. "Now? I . . . I'm not even dressed properly."

"What you're wearing is fine," I say. "There's no need to impress me." I put my arm out to her and her face flushes a little. She loops her arm in with mine and her warm, sweet scent hits me again. This time, the Triad purrs with pleasure.

"I'm ready when you are," she says.

We walk along the path towards the Royal House. I have to admit, I'm a little unnerved about it. This is the first time we'll be walking through town together, arm in arm. I don't know how we will be received.

"All of this is so different than the life that I came from," she says. "It's hard to believe that it wasn't that long ago that I was just a nurse living in my own lonesome life."

I look at her, beautiful tanned skin and shining hair. "You were lonely?" I ask. "Really?"

She smirks at me. "You find that hard to believe."

"I do. I'm surprised you weren't entertaining suitors all the time."

She shrugs a little. "Never had the time or the opportunity, I guess. I've had a pretty lonely life."

I nod, my fascination with her growing as we walk. She's not like anyone I've ever met and that does make me wonder what her life was like before she came here.

"I was an orphan, in fact," she goes on. "Bounced around from foster home to foster home until I aged out of the system. I never really had anybody."

My heart sinks a little. For all my current struggles, my youth was filled with family and light until it all went up in smoke. I can't imagine starting off life with no one.

"Hopefully, all of that will change," I say to her and she smiles gently at me in response. We walk, getting nearer to town all the time, but my worries are sidelined as I walk next to her, arm in arm.

"Can I ask you something?" she says as we reach the edge of the wood and the road leading through town.

"You may ask, yes."

She pauses and I look down at her. She's got a pensive look on her face. "We never talked about what happened to me," she says. "I mean, we've never really spoken in depth about it. I have to assume that since I'm still with the Mages, there's still danger for me here?"

I nod. There's no sense hiding that from her.

"The woman, wolf, whatever. Does she still want to harm me?"

I sigh and say, "You have nothing to fear from Natasha anymore. She is under guard."

"Under . . . you mean, she's in jail."

"Yes. At least until I decide what should be done with her. Her charge is treason, Crystal."

She goes silent. We are coming to the main road and I can already see people on the street, walking in and out of storefronts and going about their lives. My nerves are on edge, but I keep calm for Crystal's sake.

"Will she be executed?" she asks, pulling me out of my thoughts.

"Excuse me?"

"Natasha. Will she be executed?"

I furrow my brow. "It is the law that she should be. I don't know that I will follow it, however. The matter is . . . complicated."

"How?"

"Crystal, we shouldn't be speaking about it in the open."

"Is she your ex?"

I stop and stare at her. "No," I say with a laugh. "If you must know, she was the best friend of the woman I was to be mated to. That is all."

She blinks and I feel like there are a million questions behind her eyes. "It's just that . . . the things she said before she kidnapped me . . . she seemed jealous of me. I've been trying to figure out why she did what she did."

How can I explain this? How could I ever explain all of it to her? I pull her arm closer to me and I say, "It's a long story. Maybe one that I will share tonight over dinner. Maybe another time in our future. It is unimportant right now, however. Natasha is being punished for her crimes and you are safe from her. That's all you need to know."

She seems to accept that, and she doesn't question me further on the subject. We walk along the stone road leading to the palace and surprisingly, we garner no negative attention. Those who cross our paths stop and bow or curtsy. A few even utter greetings towards us.

They don't seem angry or concerned. Perhaps they silently question why I walk with Crystal on my arm, but no ire comes our way. This might be an easier time than I was thinking it would be. All I know is that this is probably the happiest I've been since Jessica's death, so . . . maybe I should stop fighting it so hard.

The royal dining room is decked out per my specifications. The long table in the center of the room is filled with food of all types—finely cooked meats and fresh vegetables and fruit picked and prepared to display the highest color and ripeness. Beneath is a fine tablecloth with the symbols of my family crest embroidered in the hem, and in the center is a beautiful centerpiece of white and gold flowers from the Mage Gardens.

"Is all this for us?" Crystal asks with wide eyes.

"Yes, of course."

She covers her mouth as she stares. Then she shakes her head and says, "This is too much food. We couldn't possibly eat it all."

"Well, I didn't know what you would prefer," I say, taking her hand and leading her to her place, the chair next to mine at the head. "So I told them to get everything."

I pull out her chair and she sits down, thanking me. I take my seat as she continues to look at the food.

Several servants come in and stand at their places in the four corners of the room. She looks around at them questioningly. "They're here to serve us," I tell her. "That's all."

She chuckles and says, "This is just too much."

"Shall we?" I ask her and she nods brightly. I wave to the servants and they step forward, preparing our plates. Two of them ask Crystal what she would like and she pauses, her eyes looking over the cornucopia, trying to decide. She does, finally, opting for the ham closest to her with the potatoes and green beans on the side.

"I don't think I've eaten this much since Thanksgiving," she says as they make her plate.

"Thanksgiving?"

"It's a holiday. We go to our family's houses and eat lots of food, basically."

I nod, but I'm a little confused. Do humans not eat with their families normally? How lonely they all must be. In a strange way, I can relate to not having had a meal with my entire family since I became Alpha King.

"So, you said that you would tell me more about Natasha," she says as the food is placed in front of her.

"Well," I say as I start on my food. "As I said, she was the best friend of my former mate."

She nods. "And she wanted you for herself once your mate was gone, right?"

I pause, but I nod just the same. "Natasha... Natasha is a complicated part of this puzzle. I don't know what her intentions were before my mate's death, but it wasn't more than a week after that she started making advances on me. I thought I'd made it clear that I did not want her to be my mate, but... apparently, I was wrong."

She nods, then asks, "How did she die? Jessica, I mean. If you don't mind my asking."

"Jessica was killed by my brother, Raphael, when I became Alpha King."

Her eyes widen and with a mouthful of food, she says, "What?"

"It was a great tragedy. You see, Raphael and I are twin brothers. For much of our lives, our births were thought to be a boon to Clarion. There was even talk about the possibility of two Alpha Kings." I smile, more to myself than to her. The memory of that time in our youth is a pleasant one. The thought of ruling with my brother at my side.

"That was not to be, however. You see, the Alpha King is chosen through a ceremony. We must stand before the Moon Goddess and ask for her approval."

She frowns a little. "So, your position isn't a matter of birth?"

"Only in the sense that royal born stand first before the altar. If for some reason a royal born is not chosen, then others may try."

"Wow," she says, her voice a light whisper. "I guess it is a good thing to have more than one child, then."

"Yes. Royal children must stand before the altar. Whoever is chosen will be the next in line." My heart aches a little at the memory of that night . . . the night before I was to be mated. Father had been so happy before we walked into the chamber, looking at us both as if this was the best day of our lives. Little did he know . . .

"It didn't work out like I hoped it would," I tell Crystal. "I was all but convinced that we both would be chosen. It had never happened in our history, but . . . it seemed logical to me. My brother was as apt to rule as I was in my mind."

"You were chosen instead of him," she says softly and I nod.

"His anger was palpable when the decision was made," I say, picking around the food on my plate. "He stormed out and my father went after him. I was so young and confused . . . I stayed with the Mages to let my father sort him out."

I set my fork down and take a drink of wine. This memory isn't easy for me to relive.

"I found my father hours later. Bleeding from a knife wound to the heart. I held him in my arms and called for help, praying that it would come in time. As I held him, my father grabbed my hand with his last bit of strength and told me to leave him and see to Jessica. *Find Jessica.* I didn't understand why at first . . . but as the Mages came in to care for him, I ran to Jessica's quarters."

I stop, my eyes burning with the coming of tears. Her warm hand covers mine as she softly says, "You don't have to go on. I'm sorry it's such a painful memory for you."

I look at her and she has tears in her eyes. I reach to her, wiping them away with my hand. "I'm sorry," I say. "I didn't mean—"

"It's fine," she says. "It's a sad story. I get it. The loss must have been terrible."

I look into her beautiful eyes and the Triad inside me rejoices. *Kiss her* . . .

I pull away and return to my food. "But enough tragedy," I say. "Tonight is not a night for tragic backstories. Since you've been here for a while now, how do you find Clarion now?"

She sits back, sniffling away the remainder of her tears and taking the new direction in conversation.

"Well, from what I've seen, Clarion is remarkably beautiful and peaceful," Crystal says with a bright smile.

"I'm glad you think so."

"It's the truth. Besides that, everyone I've met has been . . . well, wonderful in their own ways. Leslie, especially. She's become my closest confidant."

"Leslie and Hannah have always been loyal servants . . . and good, honest Mages. I trust them with my life."

"As you should. They're good people. Even Hannah." I give her a perplexed look and she rolls her eyes. "She had her reservations about me, but she is a good woman. She's treated me with dignity since the moment I was brought here. That says a lot about who she is as a person."

"I'm glad to hear you say that. Hannah took care of me after my father's death. Many times, she acted as a parent in every way that I was lacking. I owe her everything."

"I see," she says. "That explains a lot, actually. I thought that maybe she was simply loyal to your office or something. She always seems so full of pomp and circumstance. I guess it's not that at all. She's just protective over you."

I hadn't thought about that, but I guess it's true. Hannah always seems to act with my best interests in mind.

We talk a little more and we eat a little more. Being this close to her for this long is driving my Triad a little wild. As much as I'm trying to pay attention to the conversation and to her, I'm having to exert an unusual amount of control over myself.

She pushes her mostly eaten plate away and says, "I can't eat another bite. This is so much food."

"I'm glad you enjoyed it," I tell her. I don't want her to leave, but she must and soon. I feel like I'm going to jump out of my skin.

"Is it hot in here?" she asks, fanning herself. "God, it suddenly feels . . . I don't know. Like the heat's on or something."

"I don't know. I can get you something cool to drink." I wave to one of the servants. He nods without a word and fetches the pitcher of water near her.

At the same time, the doors open and Dylan walks in, then pauses, his eyes growing large. "Yes?" I ask him.

"Sire. A word, please."

"I am having dinner, Dylan."

"It is of the utmost importance."

I glare at him, more angry than annoyed. The urge to punch him for even interrupting me is unusually strong. I turn to Crystal, who's now drinking a cool glass of water. "One moment, my dear."

I follow Dylan out of the room and close the door behind me. "What is it?" I ask angrily.

He flinches a little, then, "Sire, it is getting late. You need to take refuge."

"Refuge? What are you talking about? I need no refuge."

He swallowed hard. "You must . . . and so must Crystal. It is imperative."

His eyes are shaky and the tiniest of points are coming out from his teeth. "What is the matter with you?"

I reach out to him, but he steps away. "My lord, I realize that with all that's going on, it is hard to keep track of the days . . . but I did not think you would forget what tonight is."

It only takes me a few seconds to grasp his meaning, then it clicks. It's the reason why my animals are especially restless. They've been up and down all day and within the last hour, they've been hardest to control.

It's the Blood Moon. Even the strongest of us can't resist its pull. Normally, I am locked away by this point. Kept out of sight while my primal urges rage out of control until sunrise.

But I'm not locked away . . . the object of my lust sits just beyond that door.

"Thank you for reminding me," I tell him. "I will say my goodbyes and have the Mages come for her."

I turn and walk away, but Dylan is right behind me. "My lord, no. You can't—!"

He grabs my arm to stop me. "Hannah came to me not long ago. She thinks she's found what Crystal is . . . and if she is right, you cannot go in there. Not tonight."

My heart pounds like a drum, a mix of emotions roiling inside me. "Spit it out," I growl at him.

"Hannah believes that her ability to heal so quickly and her being undetectable by any of the Mages can only be attributed by one creature. A Phoenix."

Through my boiling, lust-filled insides, a wash of cold realization comes over me. "That can't be true. There hasn't been a Phoenix for . . . for generations."

"Yes . . . but if she is one, she will be affected just as much by the Blood Moon as you. You must not go back in there."

I look at the doors. If she is a Phoenix, then she will be terrified . . . maybe even confused at what's happening. If not . . . if not, she will be wondering why I left without saying goodbye. But if I go in there, I don't know how much longer I will be able to control myself around her.

I can't just leave her. Nothing within me wants to just leave her.

I walk to the door, Dylan right behind me. "Sire, please."

I open the doors and she's standing, her eyes glowing gold and her chest heaving under her white linen gown. Her skin looks wet with perspiration as she stands there, running her hands through her hair.

"Leon . . .?" she says, her voice breathy. "What's happening to me?"

"Oh no," I hear Dylan say.

I can't fight this any longer. The logic in my mind is slipping away as I start to hear the howls of wolves within the city in the distance . . .

"Leave," I growl.

"Sire—"

"I SAID GO! ALL OF YOU!"

Dylan jumps back, then waves to the servants as they all scramble away. Crystal starts to go as well, trailing after them. As soon as she gets close to me, I stop her with my hand to her chest. The momentary feel of her breast pressing against my hand sends shockwaves through me. Her golden eyes look up at me, confused . . . then something else.

"Not you," I say to her.

Chapter Thirteen — Crystal

I was only sitting there for a few minutes after Leon left when I started to hear the howls in the distance. In those empty minutes, my body felt like it was on fire, my skin seemed to vibrate and I could feel my thighs getting slick with . . . sweat? No. Not sweat. I know that now.

Standing here so close to Leon, my body aching for his touch like never before, I know this isn't a sudden sickness or madness. It's unbridled and uncontrollable. I just want to feel him inside me . . .

"What's happening to me . . . to us?" He's snarling, his fanged teeth protruding from his mouth. My mind wanders, wondering what it would feel like to have them pierce my skin, digging into my shoulder as I come.

"It's the Blood Moon," he says. His voice is like an earthquake, rattling through my body, threatening to shake me to pieces. "It brings out the animal in me . . . brings out the passion in all magical beings."

"I'm . . . I'm not magical." He grabs me around the waist and pulls me to him. I feel his claws tearing into my gown, pressing against the soft skin of my back.

"You are," he says. "And I must mate with you."

I want to tell him no. I want to push him away. But I can't. His hot breath in my face and his mouth so close to mine. I want him. All of him. I can't stop myself.

He kisses me hard, his fangs biting into my lip as he grabs one of my breasts through my gown. *Yes, bite me, tear me to shreds . . .*

We kiss and the taste of blood mixes between us. He moves down to my neck, kissing me as I hear the fabric of my dress tearing from the back. He's ripping it right off me and I don't care. I push him away long enough to step out of the shreds of fabric, then I reach for his tunic, pulling it up so I can feel his rock-hard abs.

He helps me, pulling it all the way over his head and tossing it to one side as I kiss his chest. His hot skin against my lips as his claws move lightly down my back. I move my hands to his pants and he stops me, taking my hands and pushing them away. He takes me by the waist and leans in, his tongue hot and eager around my nipples. The excitement is killing me. My pussy throbs and my thighs are so slick with my juices. I've never come just from this, but the way this feels . . . oh God, I'm already so fucking close.

With a growl, he releases me, but only just long enough to undo his pants and take them off. My eyes drift down to his swinging cock and the part of me that's still a little rational is terrified. He's so big. It hangs halfway down his thighs. I've never been fucked with anyone so well endowed before.

"You are mine," he growls, approaching me. Instinctively, I step back from him, but he moves fast, closing the gap in seconds and presses me against the wall.

"No, wait," I whisper as he lifts me up, grabbing my legs and lifting them up so that there's nothing but the wall and the weight of his body bracing me. His giant dick is pressed against my love and I'm eager and scared all at once.

"I won't be denied," he growls as he moves his cock up and down, hitting my clit over and over. I'm so wet I can barely stand it. He slips and slides easily against me.

"I'm going to fuck you so hard and so deep," he says, "you will never want another. Tonight I will make you mine."

I bite my lip as he finally enters me. The twist of pain and pleasure explodes all at once as he thrusts hard. I cry out and stars flash in front of my eyes. I hold tight to him as he goes harder and deeper. He pushes my legs back and I dig my nails into him.

I'm only vaguely aware of Leon's animalistic groans as he holds me here, fucking me hard and deep against the wall. All coherent thought is lost as Leon exerts his control over me. My legs begin to quiver in his hands as my climax rises within me. I'm falling into this fast, my hands moving up to his hair.

"Oh fuck," I cry out, my orgasm washing over me. I come in his arms and he slows and watches me, his eyes connecting with mine.

I curse the fact that I don't have control of myself, but everything feels so much more intense than that first kiss weeks ago. Every touch of his hands feels like my skin is on fire. I can feel every ridge of his cock as it moves in and out of me, filling me up like no man ever has before.

He kisses me, devouring my mouth with so much passion and hunger that I have no hope of fighting it. He lets my legs go and I instinctively wrap my legs around his waist.

"Don't stop," I whisper. "Oh, Leon, don't stop."

He growls and lifts me off the wall, carrying me to the table. He pauses to knock all the plates and glasses away from our seats and they crash on the floor, making a loud racket. He lays me down on the table and his strokes get hard again. I reach up and run my fingers through his hair. He nuzzles my hand, the vibration of his growls against my skin.

"Oh, Crystal," he moans before he presses his lips against mine again. I moan in his mouth, my body on fire with every thrust. He kisses my chin, my throat, licks me down the valley between my breasts before taking hold of one and sucking on my hardening nipple.

His tongue roams around and around the nipple of one breast, then moves to the other. And for the moment, I'm in bliss, the feel of his tongue taking me over. Finally, he lifts up and lets his fingers flick my wet nipples, smiling down at me as he slows down again. "You are so beautiful," he says softly. "I want to fuck you all night."

I want him to. I want this between us forever.

He pulls out of me and my legs shiver with the sudden separation. Then he leans down and lifts my thighs, pulling them apart. I'm completely exposed, my sopping wet sex shining up at him. With eyes alight with passion, he leans into me, his tongue finding my clit immediately.

"Oooh!" I moan as the surprise of his hot mouth on me sends my body into overdrive. My legs start to shake again and he wraps his strong arms around my thighs to hold me firm. I grab hold of his head, my fingers entwined in his dark hair.

This is it, I'm going to come again. I moan long and loud as everything inside me breaks apart. First, his tongue flicks my swollen nub, moving around it in circles. As my moans get louder, he wraps his lips around it, sucking in quick, firm motions.

I explode and he holds on to me as my whole body vibrates. I come so hard, I can't form words. I just moan and shake against him.

When my orgasm starts to wane, he moves between my legs again, sliding himself inside me once more. I gasp, arching my back as he fucks me slowly. I don't know how much more of this I can take.

"Come again for me," he whispers. "I want to feel you explode all over my dick, baby."

I could. I might. Oh, this feels so fucking good.

I squeeze myself around his dick and his brow furrows. He sucks air between his teeth as he moves through tighter walls.

"Don't stop that," he growls. "Oh, that feels good."

I watch his eyes close, lost in the feel of my body. A low rumble of a growl comes up from him and he grabs the back of my head, pulling me into a kiss as he continues his slow moves on me.

I can feel myself about to come again. He makes it so easy for me to bend into him. As he lays me back down, he rubs my nipples between his fingers, letting them slide around from the sweat all over my body.

The look in his eyes . . . this isn't moon madness anymore. He looks at me with such reverence, his eyes move over my body like he's touching me visually as well. This king that everyone fears . . . he's worshiping my body. Worshiping me.

I lean up onto my elbows, moving my hips to match his motions, squeezing and releasing in rhythm. His moans soften to gasps, then he grabs hold of my thighs and lifts them up and back, leaning into me. He's so deep inside me right now.

His eyes hold so many sensual promises, and I don't want to let go. I look up into his eyes and he takes my head into his hand, looking down at me lovingly.

"By the Moon Goddess," he whispers, wrapping his hand around me. He leans into me and kisses me again, gentler . . . and the thought enters my mind. One that I don't know would have ever occurred to me.

I am his. Truly. Completely. "Leon," I whisper against him. "My King . . . my love . . . my Leon . . ."

"All mine," Leon responds with a grunt. His pace changes to get a little harder and I feel his body start to vibrate. I stare into his beautiful red eyes until they roll up and I feel him explode inside me. He lets out a gasping moan, whispering, "My love . . ."

He nuzzles his head into my shoulder, then I feel the slow prick and burn of his fangs as he bites me. I moan and on the edge of my last orgasm, another splits me in two as I come with him.

And somewhere outside the windows, the sound of wolf howls fades into the night as the smell of rain comes in and the first drops start to fall.

A moan escapes my lips as I slowly rise from sleep. I'm sore all over, but it's a delicious feeling. Recollection of Leon taking me over and over from last night 'til dawn runs through my mind as I roll over in his grand bed.

The madness of the Blood Moon is intoxicating. I feel like I've had way too much to drink and some of the details of last night are a little hazy... like how I got up to his room in the first place. I sit up and look around, through the intricately carved four posts of the bed and up to the high ceilings with golden trim and a mural of wolves howling at the moon above me.

This Blood Moon... I don't know what it is exactly, but I am glad I experienced it with Leon. I can't deny it any longer. We are connected somehow.

It's so strange... Up until yesterday, Leon had avoided me like the plague. And now I'm in his bed. Is this what it means to be mated to one another here? Maybe we never had a chance, despite how much we fought it.

I look over at him, asleep in the shaft of sunlight coming in through the window, the faint smell of the storm last night still coming in off the breeze. He's lying on his back, his dark hair flaring out on the pillow, and his tan skin taking on a sort of glow. I've never seen a more perfect man than him. I—

A pain in my shoulder shoots through me as I turn towards him. My hand goes up and touches the wound that's already healing. I wonder if anyone keeps bandages and antibiotics in this place or does everyone just get sent to the Mages?

I look down at my bare chest and note the streaks of red from my wound. I guess that's to be expected. Now that I know what Leon is, I guess I'm lucky to be in one piece at all.

A light tap on the door jolts me out of my thoughts. Instinctively, I pull the blanket up to cover myself and glance over at Leon, still sound asleep. Is this improper? Will whoever is on the other side of the door freak out when they see me here?

"Crystal?" It's Leslie. She's whispering as if she doesn't want to be heard. "Are you in there?"

I grab the comforter and slide out of the bed, wrapping it around me as I rush to the door. There's Leslie, staring at me with those saucer eyes.

She pauses, looking down at my nearly naked form before smiling. "I see things went well last night."

My face flushes hot embarrassment. "Apparently, it was the moon or something. We couldn't stop ourselves. Is that a regular thing around here? People just start having sex during a particular moon cycle."

"Well, yes. The wolf shifter clans, anyway. The Alpha King is a part of the werewolf clan, so he's compelled to search for his—" Her eyes fall on my shoulder wound and she gasps, hand to her mouth.

"Oh! Oh, wow, you're marked! Of course! We should have guessed it from the beginning."

"Yeah, he got a little rough." I look back to see Leon starting to stir a little. "Listen, could you get me some clothing or something? My dress got a little . . . torn last night."

"Oh, yes, yes. That's part of why I came." She reaches into her bag and produces another sheer white gown. Does no one wear regular clothes around here?

"Thanks," I say as I take it from her. "I should probably head back—"

"Oh, no, no. You're mated now, Crystal. Your place is here by the King's side until the bonding ceremony."

I blink at her in confusion . . . then I think back to all his passionate declarations. The way he growled that I was his, like he was laying his claim on me. It was hot in the moment, but . . . crap.

"In fact," Leslie adds, "if you'll let me in, I'll tend to your wound so you two can get back to getting to know one another."

I start to protest, even though I'm not sure of what I'm protesting when I hear Leon's voice.

"Who are you talking to, Crystal?"

I sigh and step back, letting Leslie in. She steps over the threshold and then bows to him briefly. "Alpha King."

"Rise," he says, waving a lazy hand at her. "Are you here for a purpose?"

She looks back at me tentatively, then to him, "Well, Mother sent me because . . . well, we're having some trouble with our crops."

"What trouble? Has something happened?"

"I know you were busy last night, my lord," she says a little softer than intended, "but . . . it rained last night."

I watch as his eyes get large for a second, then he looks away, almost as if he's ashamed . . . of the rain?

"What's going on? Why is that important?" I ask Leslie.

"Our flowers and herbs and other crops don't require very much water," she says, "as it does not rain in Clarion."

That doesn't make any sense. "What do you mean it doesn't rain? Like it doesn't rain a lot?"

She shakes her head, and it is Leon who answers, "She means that it does not rain. Ever. Unless . . ."

He trails off and I suddenly feel like I'm the butt of a joke. What the hell is going on here?

"Unless?" I urge him.

He sighs and pats the bed next to him. "Sit." I do and Leslie takes a step back as if to leave.

"Stay, Leslie," he said. "Your grasp of lore is greater than mine in places. I may need help explaining."

She remains standing, her hands clasped. She keeps her distance from us, which is odd, but I suppose it's all a part of the respect thing.

"You are what is known as a Phoenix," Leon says.

"A . . . Phoenix? Like the bird?"

"I'm not familiar—"

"It's a bird in ancient human lore," Leslie chimed in.

"Oh. Well . . . what you are is a bit different than that. You are a part of a race of supernaturals that we thought were extinct."

"A supernatural?" My mouth gets dry as I try to wrap my mind around his words. "Extinct?"

He nods his head. "A Phoenix hasn't been seen in Clarion for centuries. You are a being of great power. Some say the powers of a God."

"Whoa." I stand up and laugh a little, my nerves getting to me. "I'm no god. I'm just a normal, everyday woman. I'm not powerful."

"You made it rain," Leslie says. "The last time it rained . . . well, was before the last Phoenix died and that was centuries ago."

I can't believe what I'm hearing. I balk out loud. "You're telling me that it rained last night because of me? That I made it rain? That's ridiculous. I can't make it rain."

"You can," Leon says in a gentle tone. "And you'll soon find that you have other gifts as well."

"Mother thinks you have a gift for healing," says Leslie. "She saw it in how fast your wounds healed when you were brought here. And even now, your mark is already fading by the moment."

I look down at the wound in my shoulder. Already scabbing over and starting to itch. Leslie wrinkles her nose as she looks at it.

"We should probably still clean it up, though." She turns to Leon. "My King, might I be excused to help the mistress clean and dress her wounds?"

"Of course," he says. Leslie takes my hand and leads me away and out of the room. As we open the door, we nearly run into Dylan, who's looking at me like I've sprouted antlers. Leslie acknowledges him with a short bow.

He asks, "Is the king in his chambers?"

"Yes, he is."

"Good. Thank you."

I'm pulled away as Dylan goes into the room. Back to royal business, I guess. I start thinking about all that has been said so far. That I'm a Phoenix . . . whatever that is. And I'm "mated" to Leon. I don't know yet how I feel about that. I mean, it sounds serious. Like marriage. I don't know if I want to be married to Leon . . .

This is too much to deal with. I'm afraid of what will come next.

Chapter Fourteen — Crystal

I'm back among the Mages, dressed in my sheer nightgown, my wound cleaned, but otherwise left alone to heal on its own, which it almost completely has. I'm sitting in one of the many beautiful gardens with Leslie, picking at the itchy scabs around my wound. There are Mages all around us, digging out drenched flowers and herbs in an effort to repair the damage from the storm.

"Are you all right?" Leslie asks me. I look up from my wound. I've always told kids at the hospital not to pick their scabs. *They'll leave a scar*, I used to say. If this leaves a scar, I suppose that'll be the whole point.

"I don't know where to start," I say to her. "I'm a Phoenix . . . and I'm Leon's mate now? We were just starting to get to know each other. And last night . . . that shouldn't count. How does it count?"

"It counts," Leslie says with a shrug. "Wolves look for the mates they are fated to be with. Had you been here, the Alpha King would have come here to find you. You're supposed to be together, it seems."

"But . . . but he told me about his other mate. The one who died? If I'm fated to be his, how could she have been fated as well?"

"Who says that fated mates have to be one-to-one? Sometimes, some wolves get lucky . . . or unlucky, depending on the circumstances. I once knew of a wolf who had three fated loves. Met them all in one night."

I raise my eyebrows in disbelief. I can't even imagine that. "Wow" is all I can say. "That sounds . . . confusing and a little heartbreaking."

"Indeed. Sometimes, though, a wolf has only one mate fated to them, and if that mate was unjustly killed, the Moon Goddess may grant the living mate someone else. It's rare, but it happens."

"So . . . I'm this rare thing all the way around," I say with a shake of my head. I think about how I felt during the Blood Moon. The way my skin felt like it was on fire. And when Leon finally touched me . . .

"I'm not a shifter, though," I say. "Right? Certainly not a werewolf. So, why did the moon affect me?"

"I never said it *only* affects werewolves. Just that it does." She sighs and sets a comforting hand on mine. "Besides, you're Leon's counterpart. He went into heat, so, you had to go into heat as well. From this point on, no other will be able to satisfy you the way he did."

I wrinkle my nose. What does she know about my satisfaction? Even if that does seem kind of true. I've never had sex the way I did with Leon and I don't think I want it ever again if it's not like that.

"You know," she adds, "I believe that the Alpha King has known all along that you were his mate. Perhaps instinctively at least. Otherwise, he'd never have brought you here in the first place."

"He believes I have some supernatural powers," I counter.

"You do. You even smell different this morning."

I roll my eyes. "Come on with that. I don't have any magic."

She sighs. "Your power is starting to manifest," she says. "I can smell it on you. Soon, there's no telling what wonders you'll be able to produce."

I sigh and look up at the cloudless sky. It's curious that there isn't a single cloud now after the rain has passed.

"You know," says Leslie, standing up, "why don't you try to do something?"

"What?" I laugh.

"Don't think too hard about this. Perhaps, this is your chance for your destiny to be fulfilled," she says.

"Destiny? My life has been turned upside down."

"Allow the Moon Goddess to lead you on the right path. Live the moment," she whispers as she takes me by the hands. I take her hands gingerly, but I'm skeptical. And honestly, at this point, I just want to be at peace. I want to be happy. I release a sigh as she shakes my arms to encourage me.

"Try to make it rain," she says.

I laugh. "Leslie—"

"Just try it. Not a lot, though. I don't think Mother would forgive us for a downpour so soon."

"How is this even possible?" I say with a laugh. "I've never done magic before."

"Well, I know when I do magic, it's connected to my emotions. Anger or fear or happiness. It's all a part of making it happen. What do you think of rain? How does it make you feel?"

I sigh and look up at the clear blue sky. "I've always loved rain," I say to Leslie, letting the thought build to a warm hum in my chest. "Not that I don't love sunny skies, but rain always makes me feel calm and complete. Like I'm supposed to be here walking the earth. I always feel . . . connected to it."

She nods. "That explains why it rained when you were with the king. He made you feel complete."

Just the mention of him and the warmth inside me grows. And now . . . it's darker all of a sudden.

"Oh . . . oh, my," Leslie whispers as she looks up. I follow her gaze and see clouds gathering. The faint smell of rain in the air is starting to grow and get thick around us . . . And I feel a cool drop on my arm . . . and another . . .

"By the Moon Goddess," Leslie says in amazement as the rumble of thunder fills the sky. The workers in the garden have all stopped their work and are now looking up at the sky fearfully. And with good reason. The clouds are dark and heavy above us. It's about to storm.

"Oh!" Leslie squeals as the sky opens up and drenches us both with rainwater. She's laughing as she lets go of my hands and starts splashing in the puddles forming all around us. I watch her and laugh with her as she yells. "By the Moon Goddess! You brought the rain!"

The rain is cool and welcoming as I raise my head to the sky. As the water falls, I start to feel the rumble of thunder like a heartbeat. I reach up and touch each raindrop as it falls between my fingers.

When I open my eyes and look at my hands, I can see the water down to its molecules. Tiny lights sparking within the clear liquid. And if I let myself . . . I can make it . . . stop.

The second I think of the word *stop*, every drop of water hangs in the air, suspended in mid-fall. Leslie's standing in front of me, her hair sticking to her face and scalp as she puts her hands to her mouth in shock.

"Oh shit," I whisper.

"Don't move." Leslie steps between the raindrops, touching them gently. They burst at her touch, water droplets exploding slowly in all directions. "Tell me again how you can't do magic," Leslie says with a giggle.

I look at each raindrop, knowing and understanding that I am in control of them. More than that, I control the sky and the clouds. I can even bring lightning if I want to.

"We need to talk to Mother," she says. "She'll want to know all about this."

"Yeah, okay," I say, looking all around me. "No offense, Leslie, but I feel a little like a cat that's climbed a tree. Now that I'm up here, how do I get down?"

"Mm, okay," she says. "You made it rain. Now, just . . . make it stop."

"Just like that? I just snap my fingers and—"

The droplets all fall to the ground at once, a wash of water falling over us in a rush. We both squeal in surprise, but the rain has stopped. I look up to see the clouds receding, the rolling thunder growing faint.

Before long, the sun starts to peek out and warm the earth once more.

"Do you see now?" Leslie says happily. "Oh, Crystal, you really are a Phoenix."

I can't believe this. I can't even speak for a moment. I just look at my hands, then up to the sky and I realize that I can feel the rain . . . the clouds . . . the sun . . . I can feel it all. I am powerful. More powerful than I ever dreamed . . .

And I'm terrified. My eyes start to burn and my hands shake. Leslie's smile disappears as she sees me. She rushes up to me and takes me by the shoulders.

"What's happening to me Leslie?" I whimper as my resolve breaks.

"Shhh," Leslie says, pulling me into a hug. "It's okay. This is a lot to deal with."

I bury my head in her shoulder and cry. This is as close as I've ever been to flying without a net. I don't know what I'm going to do.

"It's all right," she whispers. "It's all going to be all right."

She holds me while I weep in her arms until finally, she says, "First things first, you need to learn how to control your powers."

I chuckle despite my tears. "Seems like I've got pretty good control already."

"Well, powers like these," she says, "they can be overwhelming. Control over the weather is a big deal, you know. Plus, there are other things that you'll need to know. Basic magic stuff and all."

I nod. "That's why you want to talk to your mother."

"She knows everything there is to know about magic." I bite my lip in thoughtful silence. I guess maybe now that I'm definitely not human, Hannah might treat me with a little more warmth. Maybe. She doesn't seem the type to give out hugs willy-nilly like her daughter.

"So, let's go," she says and starts to walk away. "You know, if we're being honest, after two rainstorms in as many days, she might already know what's going on with you."

"Maybe." We start to walk back up the path towards the caves when we hear shouting and yelling somewhere nearby. We both stop and I see alarm on Leslie's face.

"What is it?"

She shakes her head, then takes my hand. "We'd better hurry back right away—"

In a flash, a figure appears before us, seemingly out of thin air. Tall, tan, dark hair . . . Leslie throws her hands up defensively and shoots a beam of light at the figure in the path. He sidesteps the light with preternatural speed. Then, faster than I can see, he's right in front of us, towering over us.

Leslie steps in front of me. "Get back, demon," she snarls at him.

The face is so familiar to me and yet so different. He has shorter hair, but it's dark and thick, like it could be long. His jawline is square with dark stubble over it and his facial features are strikingly handsome, just darker and more sinister. He smiles slightly at us, then his eyes focus behind us. I turn just in time to see Natasha standing inches from my face. She doesn't look as sleek as she had the first time I saw her. Her hair is mussed and her clothes are in rags.

Before anyone can do anything, she waves her hand in front of us and says, "Sleep."

My eyes grow heavy and all the strength leaves my body. As both Leslie and I fall to the ground, the last thing I see is the mysterious man who looks so much like Leon . . .

Chapter Fifteen — Leon

"Where is she? Speak!"

Leslie flinches, but Hannah stands next to her, her eyes firmly on me in defiance. We're standing at the entrance to the Mage caves, the injured being carried into the entrance and the dead being taken out.

The attack was swift and precise. Dylan had only just told me that Raphael had been spotted near the royal city borders. Within the hour, my castle walls had been breached, and the prisoners were freed . . . including Natasha. By the time we realized she was gone, we started to get reports of an attack on the Mage caverns.

I got here as soon as I could, Dylan at my side. The smell of blood was thick in the air as we made our way up the walk. The bastard attacked the Mages and hurt many of them, even. So much destruction all around us as we made our way up to the cavern entrance.

And Crystal. She's all I'm thinking about. What has he done? If she's harmed in any way, I don't know what I'm going to do.

My rage surfaces as I look down at Hannah and Leslie, waiting for an answer from them. An explanation or something. The animals inside me want to take my frustration out on the both of them, but I hold them back. Hurting them will do nothing but continue the destruction that has been brought down on them.

"We do not know." It is Hannah who speaks; she holds her head up fearlessly to me. She has never cared for my aggression. "We believe they took her."

"Took her?"

She nods and says, "She and Leslie were in the garden closest to the palace when they attacked us. I've been told that the Rogue shifters ripped through here, causing chaos in the surrounding gardens while Raphael staged a search for her. When they found her, he pulled his forces back into the woods."

I look to Leslie. She and Crystal are close. She's been standing there looking as though she was on the verge of tears this entire time. If I bellow at her, she might shatter into a million pieces. I hold my anger in check as much as I can and I ask her, "Leslie, tell me what happened?"

Her large eyes shift from me to Hannah. Hannah nods to encourage her. "I have failed you, Alpha King," she says. "There was no warning of the attack. When we heard the commotion, we started running back, but they surprised us. I . . . I could do nothing. They moved too fast. And Natasha—" Her mother takes her hand, squeezing it gently to encourage her. "She performed a sleep spell on us. Knocked us out."

"A sleep spell?" Dylan asks, eyes large. "Are you sure?"

"I was awake one second and then unconscious the next. That's all I know."

Dylan and I exchange glances, subconsciously thinking the same thing. *Since when does Natasha know magic?* The stakes have gotten higher. My animals pace within me, restless with anger and fear. Crystal is in my enemy's grip. There's no telling what he will do to her.

I can't calm myself. We must search the whole of Clarion and beyond. We must find her and soon or . . . I don't want to think about what Raphael might do to her.

"Sire," says Hannah, "we will do whatever it takes to help you. A power such as hers cannot be in the hands of someone like Raphael. She is the last Phoenix. She must be saved for all our sakes."

"She will be," I growl. I know what is at stake. I know now how powerful Crystal is and what Raphael could do having her in his grip. My people are in the greatest danger now.

She is also my mate. My love. My second chance...

I cannot lose her at any cost.

"Sire," Dylan says, "I will send my forces out immediately to find her. We will scour the whole of Clarion if we must."

"Fine, do it," I say quickly.

Hannah steps forward. "We will continue our search for him through magic," she says. "But is there anything more you wish for us to do, my King? We will do whatever we can to aid you."

I look at both Hannah and Leslie, both so eager to serve. "Take care of your wounded," I tell them. "We may be entering into another war and I will need all able-bodied Mages available."

They both nod. "Yes, Alpha King."

Dylan and I walk away, bound for the palace. We will find Crystal. We must.

As we walk away, Dylan says, "You should stay in the palace, my lord."

I scowl at him. "What?"

"While we conduct the search, I mean. It is best that you stay put behind the safety of our walls."

"If you think I'm going to hide behind my guards while that bastard runs off with my mate—"

"It's not about hiding, Sire." He stops and steps in front of me, looking me dead in the eye. "Raphael is a cruel, brutish creature. He's also very calculating. Think about it. He took her before to find out what she means to you. Now that he knows, he will surely use that against you."

I stiffen. Dylan is right. I could be walking into a trap by going after him myself.

"There is no doubt that he at least suspects she is a Phoenix," Dylan adds, "but that plus her connection to you? I don't think he means to do her any harm. To do so would seal off any plan to get what he truly wants from you."

I'm thinking back to Natasha and how she told us of her pregnancy . . . and of Raphael's hope for a future with her and his child. That future clearly means my destruction, however. My animals rage inside me. I can't let him get away with this.

"What must I do, then?" I say angrily. "I cannot just stand by and let him do this."

"I'm not suggesting that you do, my lord," he insists. "Let us look for her. If we find her before he can send his demands, it will ruin his plans. We can put an end to this before he gets the chance to do anything."

I don't like that plan. Maybe it's the rage I'm feeling inside about how easily Raphael entered into my realm and took Crystal, but all I want to do is strike first at him.

I take a breath, calming my impulse to act rashly. My brother is calculating, but so am I.

"We've never been able to find him successfully," I say. "He's been in exile all this time and we haven't been able to get our hands on him. The only time we've ever been close is when he wanted us to be."

I start to pace, thinking. It was like we were fighting ghosts. He's been leading us around like fools all this time.

"Sire, what must we do, then?" Dylan asks. "We have been using all our resources to find him. We have the most powerful Mages in Clarion at our disposal, and allies all over the kingdom bring in reports daily about him and his Rogues. What more can we do?"

Dylan's right. We've done everything within our powers to find him and still my brother has eluded us for years. Of course, he has. He was once a prince. He knows how the royal pack moves. It's no wonder he's anticipated us every time.

It's time I start rethinking things. Time I stop playing into the game that he already knows and make a new one.

"Perhaps looking for him isn't the answer," I say to Dylan. "In fact, I don't think it ever was. I think it might be high time we brought him to us."

Dylan cocks his head curiously. "Sire?"

"We are going to do what we should have done in the first place," I say, walking quickly along the path. "We're going to stop playing his game and make our own rules. This ends today, Dylan. It ends today."

Chapter Sixteen — Crystal

*P*ain. It's all I can feel. My head is throbbing, like something hit me hard. I'm on the ground, dirt under my hands as I open my eyes and find that I'm surrounded by darkness.

Is this a concussion? I don't remember being hit in the head. I struggle to sit up and my wrists feel weighted down, the sound of chains filling the silence of the room. I touch my wrists only to find cold metal instead of my skin.

It all comes back to me. We were standing on the path back to the caves . . . and Natasha—

"No," I whisper weakly as I try to pull my hands out of the shackles. I yank at them and they hold me firmly. Probably bolted to the walls.

Where am I? Oh God, what is this?

"Hello?" I call with a raspy voice. My throat is sore and I'm parched. I need water, but that's the least of my concerns. I've been kidnapped . . . again. Only this time, I'm awake and it looks like they mean to hold me here for a while. I don't know how long I've been here. Hours? Days? I rub my sore head. Maybe I hit it when I was put to sleep. Dammit, being knocked unconscious isn't a joke. I could really be injured here.

"Please, somebody? I need medical attention." My voice echoes in the room, but nothing but silence greets my request. I pull myself to the wall and lean against it, pulling my knees up to my chest for warmth.

I don't know how long I lay there before I hear a door unlock somewhere to my right. A moment later, light fills the entrance of the room and a figure walks in. They're so large they block the light behind them for a moment. The door closes and I hear movement in the dark. My heart thrums in panic and I pull my legs tighter to my chest.

"Please," I say, my voice shaky with fear. "Help me."

The figure moves through the dark before walking into a shaft of light from a window somewhere high above me. I see his face clearly in the dim light and I realize that it's him. The one that blocked us on the path.

He looks like Leon. Almost exactly like him. The same height and massive shape, the same dark hair and romance-novel good looks.

Only his eyes are different. Cold and dark, like voids staring through me. He smiles at me, but it looks more like a snarl. His fangs come out menacingly with a low growl.

Like a sledgehammer, I'm hit with the memories of that night from the hospital. They rush through me like a wave. The snarl . . . the fangs . . . the growl . . .

Oh my God. He's the creature that tried to kill me months ago. And I'm trapped in this place with him.

He walks up to me and I start to shake. He squats in front of me and reaches out to touch my skin. I flinch as his rough hands graze my cheeks.

"It's good to see you again, Crystal," he says, his voice rough and cold. I can't stop shaking and I feel my eyes start to burn with tears.

"Y-you . . . you're Leon's brother," I say and his snarl widens.

"In the flesh," he says.

"Where am I?" I ask him, trying to find my courage. He says nothing. Just then, the door opens again. I turn just in time to see Natasha walk in.

"Please," I whimper.

"It's best you keep quiet," she says, leaning against the wall, her arms crossed. She's no longer in rags. She's dressed the way I first saw her. Leather tunic and pants, her dark hair pulled back and away from her face.

"Any news from the Warriors?" Raphael asks her.

She sighs, looking at her nails as if she was bored. "Everything is moving just as expected. They are all on the hunt."

He nods and looks back at me. "Good. Very good. Leon is still as predictable as ever."

"He won't stand for this," I say. "He'll kill you both when he finds you."

"He'll try," Raphael says with a laugh, "but he won't succeed. You see, now that we have you, we have him. He just doesn't know it yet."

"Please," I beg, "Raphael. Don't do thi—"

With lightning speed, he wraps his hand around my neck, pushing me back into the wall. I gasp, reaching for his wrists and digging my nails in as he strangles me.

"I am Alpha King to you!" he yells. "You will address me as such or face my wrath!"

I struggle as he slowly crushes my windpipe. I see Natasha take a step forward. "Careful," she says, "Our plan means nothing if she's dead."

His snarl fades a little and just as quickly as he grabbed me, he releases me. I fall forward, gasping for air. He stands and turns to face Natasha.

"You are correct, my love," he says. "As always."

I look up in time to see him touching her face gently. She doesn't seem so in love with Leon now. So much for that, I guess.

Raphael turns back to me and says, "You should know that Leon searches for you as we speak, but we will be ready for him when he comes."

I shake my head. Part anger and part fear fills me. "I'm bait?"

Natasha laughs. "Of course, you're bait. He thought he was going to make you Luna. He was sorely mistaken. He made the wrong choice yet again and just like the last time, he's going to pay for that."

I sit up a little, looking at Natasha's angry face. "That's what this is about for you, isn't it? Getting him back for snubbing you?"

"I'm over him," she says, stepping forward angrily. "He's nothing to me now and when Raphael finally takes his head and crowns himself king, I will be Luna the way it was always intended to be."

She starts to take another step towards me, but Raphael touches her shoulder to stop her. "Don't pay her any mind," he says. "She's only trying to antagonize you. She doesn't know that her side has already lost."

He puts his arms around her from behind, his hands cradling her stomach. He kisses her cheek and says, "We're almost at the finish line, my dear. Everything we've done will be worth it."

"You won't succeed," I say, feeling a little of my courage returning. "Leon will make sure of that."

"Yes, about that." He walks away from Natasha and squats down in front of me again. "I'll need your help to draw him to us. You know what you are now . . . don't you? Don't try to deny it. It has rained twice in Clarion. Everyone knows a Phoenix lives."

I swallow hard, looking into the void of his eyes. "So what?" I say defiantly. "It rained. Big deal. That doesn't mean anything."

His smiling snarl drops and for a second, I feel his rage. He wants to rip me to pieces. He clenches his fist and stands up, looking down at me.

"When the time comes, you will use your powers to signal to him where we are," he says, "Or I will tear out your heart and send it to him. Do you understand me?"

I nod fearfully. His snarl returns and he looks to Natasha. "Come. We've much work to do."

They leave and I'm back in the darkness. I need to get out of here somehow and fast. I need to warn Leon of what they mean to do.

I look down in the dark at the shackles and I start to wonder if somehow, these new powers can aid me somehow.

I can feel the sky outside, even in this cell. I can bring rain from here, rain with thunder and . . .

Lightning. That's it. I can bring lightning. Maybe if I aim it for my shackles . . .

God, that is so crazy. If I miss, I'll electrocute myself before I get freed. Raphael's made it pretty clear that he means to kill me either way, so what do I have to lose by trying?

The window's too high and far away from me to reach. I'd be crazy to try to stick my hand out and shock myself to get freed, even if I could reach it. I sigh, looking back down at the shackles. I can feel a little electricity in the air around me. Maybe if I . . .

I focus on the shackles, breathing in and out slowly. Somewhere in the back of my mind, there's a science class that negates what I'm trying to do. Metal's a pretty good conductor of energy. But those were the laws of physics in my old world. Clearly, some of those laws are different here in Clarion.

Before long, I feel the static in the air thickening, lifting the hair on my arms up to standing. I can see lightning strikes in my mind, and I focus on them. Just small ones. Something that might manifest from the moisture and pressure in the air around me. Something small . . .

Tiny lights start to jump from my fingertips. Oh my God. It's working!

I breathe out a long breath, pulling my focus in, focusing on the bolts holding the shackles closed. If the lights could reach the hinges . . . burn them enough to loosen them?

The light jumps from my fingertips to the bolts and the room fills with a shock of bright light. The smell of ozone fills the air as the bolts rattle, loosening in their metal cages.

"One more," I whisper and try again, this time, trying to focus the lightning to hit the hinges. "Come on . . . come on . . ."

Another tiny bolt of lightning jumps from my fingertips, hitting the hinges with a zapping noise. The metal burns away and the shackles fall off my wrists and to the ground. I almost jump for joy. I just freed myself using lightning! Hell yeah!

I get up and go to the door, hoping beyond hope that they were too arrogant to lock it. They're not. Shoot.

On the other side, I hear movement. Someone walking towards the door from a hallway. I move away, my mind spinning. Shit. I don't think I can take a werewolf.

I rush back to the shackles and put them over my hands without locking them. Maybe once the door is open, I can just bolt out of here.

I wait, the footsteps getting closer. Finally, the door opens and a thin, frail-looking woman enters with a bowl of water in her hands. There's a split second where I think maybe I ought to stick around and at least get a drink. I still feel like I haven't had water in days.

Focus, dammit.

The woman says nothing. She just bends to set the bowl down next to me. As soon as she does, I see my chance.

I leap forward, pushing her over as I shake off the shackles and run for the door. I make it out into a long hallway leading to stairs. I don't know where they go or where they will lead, but it's got to be better than being in that room.

I run for the stairs, leaping down them two at a time. I get to the bottom and I find myself in a small room with a door leading out. I rush to the door and swing it open.

Before me is a bigger room . . . with several men standing around a table. They're talking and no one has noticed me yet. One of them says, "So, the fool wishes to call you out in a challenge? This will be easier than we thought—"

He stops as each of them starts to notice me. I see Raphael standing at the far end, his eyes narrowing.

Shit. I look desperately around for an exit. There is one . . . but it's right next to Raphael.

The room fills with the sound of growling as the others glare at me, fangs bared. Raphael smiles a slow smile.

"Nice try," he says. "Natasha, if you please?"

Natasha whisks across the room and is in front of me in a second. With a smile, she says to me, "Sleep."

A familiar heavy feeling comes over me and my knees weaken. *No . . .*

I try to fight it, but the darkness sweeps around me. The last thing I hear before the darkness claims me again is Raphael saying, "Tell Leon that I will meet his challenge. Tonight."

Chapter Seventeen — Leon

The challenge has been accepted. I received word on the wind. Came back in a matter of hours. I guess I called it correct. Raphael is more bloodthirsty than calculating. If a battle is the thing that will end all this once and for all, then so be it.

Dylan stands in the moonlight with me as we watch the darkness for shadows or some sign of Raphael's forces. The moon is almost at its zenith. The battle will begin soon.

With us are my guards. All flanking out around me to protect me from any ambushes before the challenge begins. Dylan stays close, though, keeping to his job as my second.

"This is unprecedented," he says. "You cannot expect honor from Raphael, my King."

"I expect nothing from him," I say. "If he is not honorable, then we will take his head. Either way, this will be resolved tonight."

Dylan gives me a look that reads partly of worry but mostly of pride. As the Alpha King, it has and always will be my duty to defend Clarion. And that's what tonight is all about.

I look up to the moon and see that we only have seconds before it reaches its center. At the same time, we start to hear growling and sense movement in the trees around us. The air seems to vibrate and breathe on its own as our enemies approach. My Warriors shift around me, positioning themselves nervously.

"Steady," I say to them, watching the woods carefully. Then, before my eyes, the trees part and Natasha steps forward. In the company of my brother, she has cleaned herself up. Dressed in her leather garb and tied her long black hair back and away from her face. Dylan growls next to me, his animal getting riled by her insolent presence.

"Leon," she calls out. "We have come to claim your crown."

I cock my head at her. "I don't believe it was you that I challenged . . . and even if it was, you are in no condition for a battle."

She laughs. "I am protected by the true king. I fear no beast."

I begin to answer, but suddenly one of my Warriors falls forward, nearly knocking me down. I move out of the way just as bloody claws sweep forward, inches from my face.

Fury rises within me as I stare at the face of my brother. Dylan and other Warriors move forward to protect me, but I hold my hand up, smiling into the face of my brother's snarl.

"You are still as fast as ever, Brother," he says with a grin. I step back and he follows, bringing us both to the center of the clearing. My Warriors take their places as do his followers, all forming a circle around us. I glance at the fallen Warrior that Raphael has just taken out.

"Bad form attacking one of my attendants," I say, "as well as bringing a pregnant wolf to your challenge. Do you care so little for your whelp?"

"Do not speak to my Queen in that manner," he growls. "She is exactly where she is expected to be." He cocks his head at me, his eyes glowing red in the moonlight.

"But don't worry. I brought someone along to bring you a favor should you need it."

Natasha stepped back for a moment into the darkness and drags Crystal forward, bringing her into the light. She's dirty and still wearing her white Mage's gown. She looks at me fearfully, tears in her eyes.

The Triad inside me rages. It's taking everything in me not to rip her away from Natasha's grip.

"Let her go," I growl at Raphael.

"No," he says simply. "Did you really think I would show up to this challenge without bringing her? Interesting how my mate's presence strengthens me and yours only pushes you off your game. Perhaps the Moon Goddess has chosen the wrong Luna—"

"I will rip you apart if you have harmed her," I say, stepping forward. He laughs.

"I would never harm the Last Phoenix, dear brother!"

My anger takes a back seat to cold fear. We suspected that he knew what she was, but only suspected. He reads my face and his smile broadens.

"Yes, Brother. I knew about her. I've been searching for her. Why do you think I attacked her in the first place?"

I don't answer him. My stomach twists as I realize that perhaps I'm the one who has miscalculated. He starts to walk slowly around me and I match him so that we're circling each other.

"Everything is working according to my plans, Brother," he says, "Even this challenge that I'm sure you believed you thought of. I knew you would grow weary of chasing me. I knew that you would eventually call me into a challenge. In your mind, you probably thought that you were going to tear me apart here. Simple brutality. That was your whole plan, wasn't it?"

"Why don't you shift and we can find out?"

"Oh," he says with a chuckle, "so eager to die. For years, I've been trying to take back what rightfully belongs to me. Don't you think calling you into a challenge has crossed my mind repeatedly? Alphas are strong creatures . . . and even stronger once they have been gifted the Triad. How would my wolf fair against your lion? Or your bear? I would be a fool to be here without some aid. Some trick . . . some power greater than all of us."

My blood runs cold. *No.* How could I have not seen it?

"It seemed an impossible task. I thought that we would be locked in this battle of cat and mouse for ages. Then, I recalled one of our childhood stories. The Phoenix . . . who can control the weather, move the air and the earth if they so desire. They have the power of a god . . . what better way to destroy an Alpha King, gifted by the Moon Goddess?"

He stopped and faced me, his eyes glowing triumphantly. "I may not have gotten gifted by the Moon Goddess, Brother. But when I found Crystal . . . your sweet Crystal, I realized that perhaps the Moon Goddess had gifted the both of us after all. That was your wish when we were boys, wasn't it? That the both of us receive her gift. Well, it's taken many years, but it seems that your prayers were answered."

"You didn't have to involve me," I say angrily. "You could have taken her yourself back to Clarion. Why did you involve me?"

"How else was I to awaken her powers? Crystal is the bloodline of the oldest and purest of Mages. Her powers rival that of a deity. You carry the Triad, the ultimate gift from the Moon Goddess. Drawing you to her was the only way to spark her into awakening as a Phoenix. I attacked her and made sure that you could track me to her and the rest is, as they say, history." He glances over at her. She is now kneeling next to Natasha, weary from all she'd been through.

"Regrettably, I did not know she would be fated to you," he said, his smile fading a little. "But I guess we can chalk that up to a happy accident. The irony of you being destroyed by your second mate after losing your first is intensively gratifying."

"You bastard." I can feel my Triad pushing for me to shift. To rip him apart. I'm trying to hold on. I need to keep my wits about me. He throws out a laugh, the sound irritating me to the bone.

"If only," he says. "Let's face it, Leon. You are here tonight because you are weak. You always were. You come running to her rescue, letting your beasts guide you instead of the other way around. You challenge me without giving any thought to what I have in my corner. You are predictable and weak and you are nothing."

"I am the Alpha King," I snarl at him. "And you are just a whelp trying to use someone else to fight your battles."

"The fight will be short," he says. "I can assure you of that."

He walks over to Crystal and yanks her up by her hair. My claws and fangs come out before I can stop them. He's dragging her into the circle with us.

"What are you doing?" I snarl, barely able to hold myself back.

He pulls out a blade. It shines under the moonlight above us as he presses it against her neck.

"Stop me from killing her," he says. "Bring your beasts. Bring your rage. Stop me. Now, great Alpha King."

He presses the blade against the skin of her neck and she winces. I can't hold back any longer. He must pay for this.

My bear is the one that bursts forward. When I shift, the pain of it rips through me in a sort of catharsis, breaking, bending, and reshaping my bones and my muscles so I grow large and ferocious.

I am the bear and I roar so great that it shakes the trees around us. Raphael laughs while Crystal screams and starts to struggle.

"No!" she says as he holds her firm, the knife managing to slice a little bit of her neck. "Stop!"

I'm moving before I know what I'm doing, everything moving in slow motion. I don't even see Crystal anymore. Only Raphael matters. Only he will catch my wrath.

I stand on two legs, my teeth bared, my claws ready to rain down on them and the air is split with a blood-curdling scream. The last thing I see is Crystal's eyes as they glow gold. A flash of light engulfs everything and throws me backward, electricity shocking me hard.

As I fall back to the ground, I shift into human. I look up to see that the circle has been broken; all my Warriors and all Raphael's Rogues have fallen back, stunned by the blast. I look over at Raphael, who lies near the trees, stunned with blood coming from his head.

And Crystal. My dearest love stands in the center, looking down at her shaking hands. I get to my feet and stumble over to her, doing my best to stay standing. She looks up at me, and her eyes widen.

"Leon!" she weeps. "Oh God, are you all right? I didn't hurt you, did I?"

I take her face in my hands and kiss her deeply. "You only defended yourself, my love," I say.

"So she did," Raphael says as he pulls himself up to standing. "So, let's finish this once and for all, shall we?"

"I push Crystal behind me. "No tricks," I say. "This is about you and me. Let it end that way."

Raphael spits blood on the ground and takes off his cloak. "So, let it end."

He shifts into a wolf and I do the same in turn. Let the battle begin.

Chapter Eighteen — Crystal

Everything in me wants to help Leon. I can't believe I tried to hurt him. I can't believe my powers just jumped out that way.

But that was Raphael's plan all along. Get him to attack me and get me to kill him. It didn't work, however. Leon seems fine, while Raphael was blown back into a tree.

Not that that has stopped anything. The two of them shift as wolves and start to fight. Snarling hatred between the two animals, then teeth and claws, ripping away at fur and flesh. Everyone else has gotten to their feet to cheer them on. I just stand there in terror, praying that Leon isn't killed before my eyes.

What will I do if he dies? I can't control my powers that well. They will kill me. They most certainly will kill me.

But not right now. No one does anything as the two of them fight in front of us. Leon said it was between them, and everyone seems to respect that. I start to edge away from the Rogues, towards the side with Dylan and Leon's men. Natasha sees me almost instantly and rushes to me, wrapping her arm around my neck and yanking me backward.

Leon pins Raphael, his claws on his neck and his great heavy body holding him in the dirt. Natasha screams out, bringing her arm up sharply, strangling me.

"Leon!" she yells; then she says in a dark, disrespectful tone, "Look to your Luna!"

His head turns and the moment he sees me in danger, his snarl disappears and I think I see fear in his wolf eyes. Raphael pushes him off and rolls towards his clothes while Leon starts moving slowly towards Natasha.

I hear her breathing start to quicken as she moves back from him. Then she shouts, "No! I will not release her. She dies tonight, Leon."

Coward. I feel anger well up inside me. There is a burst of something I can't explain from within. I shut my eyes as it flows through me. Suddenly, I feel light. I try to open my eyes, but it's impossible. I feel myself being lifted from the ground. Pain tears from my arms, forcing me to open my eyes. I glance at them and realized my arms are no longer there. In their place are two wings, large and feathered and so white that they seem to glow in the moonlight. I look down and realize I'm above everyone. My body doesn't feel like itself. I don't know how I got so high or how I will get back down.

My eyes zero in on the most important person to me, Leon. He sees me, and then he turns as Raphael rushes him. Raphael is in his human form, naked as he charges Leon, the silver blade he meant for me in his hands.

No! I want to scream to stop it, but it's too late. Leon tries to move out of his way, but Raphael's blade is swift . . . and strikes true. He plunges it into Leon's chest. Leon brings his claws up and rips away Raphael's throat with one swipe, knocking him back and into the dirt before he falls to his knees and then to his side.

I lose myself as a scream tears from my throat. I sweep down to him on my wings, landing at his side as his body shifts back to human in the growing pool of blood beneath him. The power that overcame me falls back, giving me my arms back as I lift him up into my arms.

"Leon," I whisper as I pull him onto my lap quickly. Raphael's dagger still in his chest, his eyes fluttering, I can feel the life force draining out of him.

I want to pull the knife out, but I know I can't. He needs a hospital or . . . or a Mage or something. He needs help.

Howls sail up to the sky all around me. I look up in time to see everyone shifting into beasts around us, a new battle forming from the loss of Raphael . . . and maybe Leon. *Oh God, Leon!*

Leon stares at me with half-closed eyes. My heart breaks as he reaches out to cup my cheeks.

"Stay with me, please," I plead as my eyes burn with tears. I watch the light slowly fade from his eyes. "We'll get you help. Please, just hang in there."

He smiles, looking around at the fighting that has erupted around us. "I'm afraid it's too late for that, my love."

"No," I say, shaking my head as the sobs come up from my belly. "Please . . . Leon, don't leave me."

"I have been blessed twice by the Moon Goddess," he says in a weak voice. "Now, I must join her. Perhaps that is my final blessing."

"Don't talk like that. I'm going to get you help. You have to hang on."

He takes my hand, squeezing it against his soaked chest. "You will always be my love," he says, "here and in the beyond. I shall wait in the stars for you."

Tears fall from my face and onto his as his eyes finally shut . . . and I can feel him no more. A primal scream erupts from me, rising up above the sounds of the fighting, shaking the trees around me down to their roots. Everything stops as clouds roll in, blocking the moonlight.

With shaky hands, I pull the knife out of him and toss it aside, then I pull him into me as thunder rolls above me.

The fighting around me has stopped. Maybe they are retreating. Maybe they're all dead. I don't know and I don't care. My love is gone. My Leon is gone . . .

I weep and the sky opens up. Rain pours down on me as I rock back and forth with him in my arms, crying out in the rain as lighting cracks the sky open above me.

All hope is lost. He's gone. He's really gone.

There's a low hum all around me and I feel like there's way too much light suddenly. It's daylight . . . from where?

My tears hang in my eyes as I look up to see that all the shifters, Rogue and Warrior alike, are staring at me. I look down to see my arms and shoulders are glowing gold . . .

The gold light moves from me and to Leon, encompassing him entirely. I watch in awe as the wound in his chest slowly closes . . . and his mouth falls open to take in air.

"Leon?" I say. I lay him back down on the ground. The color slowly returns to his face and his eyes flutter. His head lolls one way and then the other, then finally, his eyes open again.

"My word . . .," Dylan says as he steps forward.

Leon looks over at him and frowns a little, then he looks back at me. "What . . . what happened?"

He tries to sit up, but I stop him. "Lie still," I say. He scowls a little and continues to sit up.

"I'm okay," he says. He looks down at his chest, the leather torn and still covered with fresh blood.

"He . . . stabbed me . . . Raphael . . ." He trails off, looking past Dylan to his brother lying in the dust, his eyes open and his throat shredded and bleeding into the ground.

Dylan kneels down on the other side of him and asks, "Are you . . . well, my King?"

Leon doesn't answer at first. He just stares at him before saying, "I think so, I . . ." He looks at me and asks, "Did you save me?"

"I think so," I say with a little laugh.

He smiles and pulls me into a kiss. "My love," he whispers. "You brought me back."

"I beg your pardon, my lord," Dylan says, "but the Rogues have all run into the woods. Shall we pursue?"

"Yes," he says.

Dylan blinks. "Will . . . will you be all right?"

He laughs. "I've never been better, Dylan."

"Then your wish is my command, Sire." He stands and turns to the remaining Warriors. "You heard your king. Find the Rogues."

They all let out a howl and shift, running into the woods, except Dylan. He stays behind as I help Leon to his feet. We're both standing and smiling at one another, ready to go on the next great adventure. Then the ground tilts one way . . . then the other. Leon's smile fades.

"Crystal?"

Before I can respond, darkness sweeps in all around me and I fall to the ground . . .

Chapter Nineteen — Leon

These last few days have been surreal. I'm thinking it all over as I sit by Crystal's bedside. She rests in my room at the palace, her place as far as I'm concerned, but she hasn't awakened since she passed out at the clearing. For three days, I have kept vigil here.

All the events leading to this moment run through my mind. My plan to challenge Raphael almost failed but succeeded when his own brutishness led to his decision to attack me. I wonder what might have happened if Crystal had not been what she is. I would have regretted allowing myself to get so angry that she got harmed. I never would have forgiven myself.

Raphael knew she would defend herself. Bet on it, in fact. And he lost out. Now, he is dead while I live. Despite it all, I have won the challenge with Raphael and I have Crystal to thank for it. As for his army of Rogues? They have all been either killed or captured except one. Natasha. She still lives somewhere on the outskirts of Clarion. I have not called any of my forces off. Should they find her, she will meet her end.

Until then, I know not if she will ever show her face again or look to seek revenge for the murder of her mate. And right now, I don't care. All I can see is Crystal. All I hope for is for her to wake up.

As I sit here, I think of her at the moment she displayed her true form. Breaking free of Natasha and rising above us all, a glorious winged creature, glowing gold and white above us. I have read that witnessing a Phoenix spread its wings is the closest that a person will ever come to witnessing a god . . . and now I know that is true.

I take her hand and I lean my head against it. Clarion cannot lose her. *I* cannot lose her. I don't know what I will do if she does not wake. Even though Hannah has assured me that she will.

"She just expended a great deal of energy," she said before she left to go back to the caves. "I will check in with you in a few days but do not worry. She is born to rise."

I smile to myself, laying my head at her side. What a wonderful way to say it. *She is born to rise.*

More beautiful than anyone in Clarion, more powerful than any Mage that lives . . . she is my Luna. My Queen. And she must awaken. It's my last thought as my eyes grow heavy and I fall asleep.

"He looks so tired."

"He has not left your side since we brought you here."

My eyes open the instant I hear Dylan's voice. I look up to see Crystal looking back down at me, a sleepy smile on her face and her hand in my hair.

"Crystal," I whisper, taking her hand in mine as my heart leaps in my chest. She is awake, finally!

"By the goddess," I whisper, pulling her into my arms. She wraps her arms around my neck and I kiss her, tasting her sweet lips once more.

Dylan, whose been standing next to the bed the whole time, clears his throat and says, "I shall take my leave, then." He bows to us both. "Alpha King. Luna."

As he leaves, Crystal smiles a little. "Luna," she says as if tasting the word for the first time. "That's me, huh?"

I nod. "Or rather it will be. We must be bonded in the name of the goddess . . . but that is only a technicality. Already everyone recognizes you as mine . . . and me as yours."

There's a part of me that worries that she will reject me. Her will and mine haven't exactly made this journey an easy one, after all.

But her smile remains and she looks me over, her eyes examining my face as if trying to record every detail.

"I don't know what happened," she says. "I . . . I guess I must have passed out. How long was I asleep?"

"Three days."

"Three . . ." She gapes for a moment, then puts her hand over her mouth. "Oh, wow. I was out for three days??"

I nod. "Hannah said it was normal."

"Huh. Okay, I guess it is?" She laughs a little. "Being a Phoenix is going to take some getting used to."

"You have time. All the time in the world."

She leans her forehead against mine and closes her eyes, breathing me in. "Thank heaven, you're all right," she says softly. "I thought . . . I don't know what I thought. I'm just so happy you're here with me right now."

"As I am with you," I say back. I kiss her and feel her warmth filling me as her hands move to my face. I am filled with love for her . . . my joy rising to the rooftops.

I lean into her, my hands moving down to her breasts, squeezing them through her gown. She smiles against my mouth.

"Leon, I just woke up," she says. "Is this . . . safe?"

"You are the greatest healer in the land," I say. "Should our lovemaking be too ardent, I doubt I am capable of harming you. I should worry more for myself."

She laughs loud and bright, then wraps her arms around my neck and pulls me down to the bed with her. Our lips connect again, our tongues twisting up in each other. She lifts her gown as I pull down my pants, already hard and eager to be inside her.

"Slow down," she whispers. She bites my lip as my cock rubs along her thigh. The animals within me are circling. Waiting for me to lose control.

"Yes, My Queen," I whisper. "Whatever you wish."

I roll over on the bed, pulling her on top of me. She straddles me, moving her hips slowly over my cock, teasing me. She's already so wet. I'm dying to be inside her. I watch as she pulls her gown down over her shoulders. The material comes down over her breasts. I take each one in my hands, running my fingers over her hardening nipples.

She's hot and dripping between her legs. I want to be inside her desperately. She leans into me, her breasts brushing my lips. I take one in my mouth, my tongue circling the nipple. Soft moans escape her as she cradles my head.

I can't take it any longer. I grab hold of her hips and angle myself inside her, sliding into her tight, wet sex as I continue to suck her breasts. Her body shivers under my touch, her moans shaky and excited.

"Oh, yeah," she whispers. "Just like that . . . yeah . . ."

I move slowly and methodically, my own moans starting to turn to growls as my claws come out and pierce the skin of her hips. She gasps and I stop, looking up at her questioningly.

"Don't stop," she says, "I can take it."

She sits up and moves her hips with mine. I thrust harder . . . faster, watching as her breasts bounce before me. The beast in me starts to come forward, fangs cutting into my lip as I get close.

"My love," I moan. "My eternal love . . ."

She squeezes around me and my body starts to shake. I pull her down, wrapping my arms around her, my claws digging into her sides. She grabs me by the hair, biting my ear as my climax climbs to the surface. "Fuck me," she half gasps, half moans. "Oh, yeah, fuck me . . ."

The sound of her voice, desperate and passionate, sends me over the edge as her legs shake and she melts into my arms.

"Oh, Leon," she says in a raspy moan. "God, I love you so much."

I turn her over, lift her legs to my shoulders and thrust deep inside her. She grabs my forearms, digging her nails into them. I look down into her dreamy eyes as her forehead furrows, her lips opening slightly with her moans.

"I love you," I say to her and she smiles, squeezing herself around me again.

"I love you," she moans.

I lean in, her flexibility giving way so that I may kiss her once more and breathe in her floral scent. The great Phoenix of Clarion is mine, and this moment is ours.

Epilogue — Leon

"May the Moon Goddess bless you, Luna!" I smile at the excited two-year-old as he runs to keep up with the carriage. The celebrations have begun all over Clarion. Bells toll our arrival as we ride back from our binding ceremony and the streets are filled with well-wishers throwing white rose petals our way to bless our union.

I look over at Crystal, perfect in her white gown, clingy and satin with thin straps so that her creamy white shoulders are on display. She is a vision. A work of art. We are supposed to greet our adoring public at the end of this ride, but I look at her and other plans form in my mind.

"That is Adro," Dylan says from the opposite side of the carriage. "He broke limbs into two while playing. Isn't that right, my Luna?"

I was so busy admiring my bride I'd forgotten Dylan was sitting with us. Crystal smiles at him and nods. "That's right," she says. "Came into the Mage caves about a week ago, I think."

She's been working with the Mages since she awoke a few weeks ago, with barely any time to plan our bonding. She once told me that she was a healer in her past. How ironic that she gets to return to what she did before. She leans a little towards me, giving me a view of her cleavage as she looks out of the window.

"His arm looks good," she says.

"It should," I respond. "The Phoenix Queen of Clarion healed him after all."

Her face flushes a little as she sits back. "I don't think I'll ever get used to that."

I take her warm hand in mine. I want to get her back home. Do away with all this pomp and circumstance and have my way with her as soon as we are indoors. She seems to sense my urge. I see her give me a sly smile as I touch her.

"By the way," Dylan says, "the ceremony was beautiful. The most beautiful I've ever seen, in fact."

Crystal raises an eyebrow at him and says, "You don't have to kiss up just because I'm queen now."

He chuckles and says, "I mean it. You are a vision, my queen. The very picture of royalty."

I glance at the position of the sun and sigh. "How long is this carriage ride?"

"Patience," she says, nudging me. "All good things come to those who wait."

"It won't be long before we're in the center of town," Dylan adds. "Then a short speech and off to the palace."

"Wonderful," I respond dryly. At her touch, my Triad awakens, purring and hungry for her love. I'm already imagining my hands up her dress and my tongue in her mouth.

To Dylan's credit, the ride isn't very long. I wave to my subjects as does Crystal. When we step out of the carriage, they will try to touch her hands, try to touch mine. It's considered good luck to touch the bride and groom right after a bonding.

Finally, I feel the carriage slow as we reach the center of town. Dylan pulls down the shades of the carriage and says to Crystal, "Don't worry about anything when you get out there. Your subjects will just be excited to meet you finally. You are protected at all times."

The tone of his voice sounds like he's more nervous than we are. Crystal scoffs. "I'll be fine, Dylan. Don't worry."

"Good. All right. Give me a few minutes to introduce you, then."

He gets out of the carriage and she turns to me, her smile turning in a little. "What?" I ask.

"I've been waiting all day to tell you this. You know, after I woke up, you had Hannah examine me to make sure everything was okay?"

I nod, tilting my head a little. She looks pensive. Maybe a little nervous.

"Well," she says, "as it turns out, I'm better than okay. Well . . . we are anyway."

She takes my hand and puts it on her belly. The implication hits me like a sledgehammer. "You . . . you are . . . pregnant?"

She nods. I pull her into a kiss, my lips joining with hers with all the passion I have inside. I pull away from her and I touch her stomach delicately. I can't believe that she's carrying my cub. She places her hand over mine, my hand against her warm, soft belly.

She is a wonder . . . I am filled with more love for her than I could have ever thought I possessed.

Crystal touches my face gently and gives me a sly look before reaching over and locking the carriage doors.

"What are you doing?" I ask with mild amusement.

She turns to me and kisses me again, taking my face in her hands and pushing me back on the seat, straddling me. When she pulls away, her eyes smolder with love and passion.

"You're all I've ever wanted," she says softly. "The people can wait a little bit while I have you to myself, can't they?"

I smile. Her thoughts are blissfully in sync with mine. We hear the muffled tones of Dylan as he goes on with his speech and I remember my responsibilities . . . but I'm looking up into the face of my love. My love who carries our future within her. "We have to say something to the people," I say a little playfully. "We can't just—"

"Are you the Alpha King or are you the Alpha King?" she says firmly, her lips turning up in a lustful snarl. "We answer to no one but the Moon Goddess herself . . . and I don't think she would mind it if we stole a single moment from this day."

My hand moves up her thighs, under her dress and around the folds of her firm backside. "I'm gonna need more than a moment, my Luna."

"As you wish, my love."

We kiss passionately and I pull the damp fabric of her panties to one side as she undoes my pants. Dylan's going to be so pissed in a few minutes.

It's not long before I'm inside her and the carriage is rocking from side to side as we make love. She giggles as we collectively hear applause around us.

"I think Dylan might be done with his introduction."

I pull her face down to me and kiss her long and deep. "Let him stall."

She smiles and I smile with her. My love, my Luna, my life . . . and this is just the beginning.

Did you like this book? Then you'll LOVE ***Alpha's Arranged Marriage***!

I never wanted an arranged marriage to a stubborn but scorching hot alpha. Fate has other plans.

Turn the page for a special preview.

Special Preview — Alpha's Arranged Marriage

Thea

The world comes back to me, and I'm met with those eyes again. I look over to see him looking down at me. He's focused on me with a deep-set frown on his face. The man from my dreams looks pissed.

"She's awake."

The tone of those two words does not inspire confidence.

A middle-aged man in a white lab coat suddenly comes into my line of sight.

"Welcome back," he says in a bright voice. "It's good to see you here and alive." He's smiling at me, but I just stare skeptically. I refuse to believe that I'm out of danger yet. I won't let my guard down so easily. The past few hours have not been kind to me.

Wait. How long has it been since the people from the vehicle grabbed me off the street? I don't even know how long I've been missing. Surely, my coworkers will be looking for me by now.

I start crying. I don't know where I am or how long I've been here. I don't even know who these people are.

"Hey, hey. You're all right. You're safe." The doctor's voice is soft as he leans closer to comfort me. I try to move away, but he remains close. "I promise you. You are safe here. No harm will come to you."

If this is still a dream, I really want to wake up from it. It's gone on for much too long.

The doctor pulls a chair up to me, and I notice I'm lying in a bed. The room is mostly white, but it's not a hospital . . . I don't think.

"You were injected with an unusually high dosage of poison," he explains. "The amount was more than . . . well, more than most people could withstand. You were able to survive, but I imagine you don't feel too great right now."

I shake my head. Now that he mentions it, my stomach feels sick. Like I had bad sushi.

A nurse comes in, and the man from my dreams steps out of the way so that she can hand the doctor a vial. "This should ease your nausea," he says and injects it into my arm before I can react. A warm feeling travels up my arm, and a second later, the nausea disappears.

Dream Man leans against the far wall, watching and frowning silently. For a handsome man, he sure frowns a lot. Or maybe the frown brings out his beauty.

"Who are you people?" I ask, my voice comes out croaky. "I can't still be dreaming, right?"

"Here, take gentle sips." The nurse is on the other side of me with a small cup and a straw.

I slowly lean up so I can drink what I hope is water. It certainly tastes like it, and my throat is soothed.

A rough scoff comes from Dream Man.

"You have got to be kidding me," he mutters and shakes his head. *What's he got to be so hostile about?*

My gaze shifts from him to others in the room to see if anyone has noticed how angry he is at me. No one's said anything. How rude is this guy?

"If you understood how my day has been," I snap at him, "you might be a little kinder. Being rude is really uncalled for right now."

It's like I dropped a bomb in the middle of the room. Both the doctor and the nurse freeze, eyes wide and fearful. The doctor dares a look back at Dream Man, who narrows his eyes as he stands up from the wall.

"You would do well to watch your tone," he growls at me. "I am Lord of this region. You will respect me."

"Respect is earned," I shoot back at him. He walks toward me, and the doctor tries to intervene.

"My Lord, please—"

"I am yet to see or understand why you are the Chosen One," he says through clenched teeth.

That phrase again. What in the world does that even mean? "You know, I don't know what you're talking about," I snap back at him, refusing to cower in his presence, "but so far, everybody that's called me that has only wanted to kill me. I'm starting to think that it's some kind of insult."

"You are a fool," he scoffs. "A silly girl from the outer lands. All these years of ancient wise men and seers, Shamans and Mages, all searching for *you*? It's ridiculous. You are clearly some kind of fraud."

My mouth hangs in shock. A *fraud*!

He turns to leave. "Fuck off, Fancy Pants," I spit at him. He whirls around.

This time, the doctor speaks up before Dream Man can do anything, "My Lord, please. You should probably let us handle this for now."

He glares at me, silvery blue eyes raging with anger. "Fine. I need to speak with Mother and the seers about this travesty anyway."

As he leaves, all I can think is *What in the ever living hell is going on, and why have I been thrust into the middle of it?*

"I am sorry," the doctor says after he's gone. "This is a . . . tense situation. I do apologize for Lord Xander's behavior."

I scoff. "Don't apologize. That guy's a dick."

"That *guy* is our Alpha, my dear. What he says goes around here."

I huff bitterly. The nurse excuses herself, and I glance over at the doctor. "What's your name, doc?"

He smiles gently. "I am Cid Olcan. I serve as the healer for Crescent Pack. The nurse that was just here is Rudy. She will be back with some medication to help you rest while your body heals."

I nod. I'm grateful for some explanation, even though that wasn't a lot at all. Ugh, I feel like I've slipped into Wonderland.

"So, you said I was poisoned?"

He nods. "It's really a miracle that you are alive. But then, if it is true that you are the Chosen One, well, then it is no miracle at all."

"Can you tell me what this Chosen One business is all about?"

Rudy came walking back in with a needle in hand. She starts injecting it in the IV drip by my bed. "I could not explain it properly," Dr. Olcan says. "The lore of it all . . . Well, it was just told me as a boy, as it has been for many of us. Just know that you are very special to us, and it is very important that you stay alive."

Xander

I still can't see it. I just don't see what others are seeing, and I can't imagine how she could possibly be the Chosen One.

By the time we brought her back, word had already gotten out that the Chosen One was among us and that we would all be saved. In town, everyone's been walking around with smiles on their faces, the cloud of doom that has been looming over the townspeople's heads for the past few years starting to fade away.

Everyone's hopes have been lifted. Except mine. But then, I'm one of the few who've actually met her. I should be the one most convinced, and I'm not. Maybe it's because I'm the only one who has lost so much already. I can't really bear to lose more.

Her insolence plagues me. I had to walk out of the infirmary before my wolf came out and ripped her to bits. I see nothing special in this girl. She's merely a random human who just so happened to be picked up off the streets and brought to Clarion. Even though the seers have confirmed who she is, I can't come to terms with it.

Why does it have to be this way?

"Did you plan on telling me, or was I just supposed to find out through gossip?"

My pace is stopped as Rhiannon's voice echoes around me in the hall. I turn to see her standing at a corner of the hallway, arms crossed, eyes blazing with anger and hurt.

I don't have anything to say. What can I say? I won't deny that I delayed speaking to her. I'm still trying to cope with it myself. She uncrosses her arms and steps up to me.

"Was that why you didn't take me with you on the rescue mission?" she asks. "Because of her?"

I want to wrap my hands around her beautiful face and tell her that it'll be all right. Tell her anything to ease her mind. But there isn't a single thing I can say that will remove the fact that I am fated to another.

"I am sorry," I say, doing my best to keep my own anger and rage out of my voice. "I never planned for any of this to happen—"

"You don't have to marry her," she says with water standing in her eyes. "You are the Alpha of this pack and this region. You . . . you can make whatever rules you want. We don't have to do this."

My mouth went dry. "But we do. Rhiannon, you have to understand, as the Alpha there have to be sacrifices. The pack comes first. My region comes *first*. You understand that, don't you?"

"Yes." Her voice is starting to break. "Yes, but not like this." She walks toward me and puts her hands on my face. I inhale her scent, the memories of our love rising up within me.

"I love you, Xander," she says, tears rolling down her cheeks. "I have loved you since we were children. Do you not love me?"

"Of course, I love you."

"Then let's leave. We can go somewhere else where no one knows us and build the family we both want. Let's leave this cursed place and start over. Somewhere far from Clarion altogether."

"We cannot leave," I tell her. "This pack . . . our families are here. We cannot abandon them. Not at any cost."

"You are the only thing I want. How can you expect me to go on serving this pack as I watch you live your life with another woman? You cannot ask that of me."

"I cannot turn my back on my pack, Rhiannon. You know me better than that."

Her nostrils flare. She steps away from me and says, with so much anger, "Fine. Do what you want. Go be with your Chosen One, and I hope you have a better life with her." She turns and stalks away from me.

I watch her leave until she's out of my sight. Then, I turn and walk away, my mind starting to spin. I have duties to attend to and, perhaps, I can also find a loophole to get me out of this disaster.

***

Alpha's Arranged Marriage is now available on Amazon!

Free book from Ariel Renner

Want more paranormal romance & fantasy romance from Ariel Renner? **Get a free novella** when you sign up for her email newsletter!

Scan the QR code above or go to:
arielrenner.com/pb-free-book

About the Author

Ariel Renner became enchanted by Disney fairy tales at an early age. Anime, Marvel comic books, and love songs on the radio further fueled her fascination with magical worlds, superhuman abilities, and happily ever afters.

She published her debut novel, *Forbidden Ice Prince*, in March 2023. Ariel loves crafting spellbinding tales of enemies-to-lovers, destiny, strong heroines, fiercely protective heroes, epic battles of good versus evil, and true love. Through her books, she hopes to offer a unique twist for fans of paranormal and fantasy romance.

Ariel lives in Frisco, Texas with her husband and their beloved corgis. When she's not writing, she enjoys traveling, binge-watching crime dramas, and filling her home with pop culture collectibles.

Discover more of her books at: **arielrenner.com/books**

Printed in Great Britain
by Amazon